Sandcastle
and Other Stories

Justin Bog

green darner PRESS

On the Beach of Ashbury, painted by the artist, George Bogdanovitch, Justin's father.

Sandcastle
and Other Stories

Mary Lou,

Hope these tales bring you laughter in the Darkness... shivery characters... love your support..

love,
Justin Bog

green darner PRESS

Published by Green Darner Press
9600 Stone Avenue North
Seattle, Washington 98103

Green Darner Press is an imprint of Gemelli Press LLC.

Sandcastle and Other Stories
By Justin Bog
Copyright 2013 Justin Bogdanovitch.

Cover design and typesetting by Enterline Design Services LLC
Author Photograph: Christa Gallopoulos and Chris Kresge

ISBN: 978-0-9884784-1-1
Library of Congress Control Number: 2013930681

All rights reserved. No part of this book may be reproduced, stored in a retrieval system or transmitted in any form or by any means without the prior written permission of the publishers, except by a reviewer who may quote brief passages in a review to be printed in a newspaper, magazine or journal. This book is licensed for your personal enjoyment only. This book may not be re-sold or given away to other people. If you would like to share this book with another person, please purchase an additional copy for each recipient. If you're reading this book and did not purchase it, or it was not purchased for your use only, then please return it and purchase your own copy. Thank you for respecting the hard work of this author.

Sandcastle and Other Stories is a work of fiction. Names, characters, places, and incidents either are a part of the author's imagination or are used fictitiously. Any resemblance to actual persons, living or dead, events, or locales is entirely coincidental.

The cover art is a detail taken from one of my father's paintings. His paintings, as well as my mother's art, can be viewed at www.bogdanovitch.com. The book cover design was completed with help from the incredible talent at www.convenientintegration.com. I highly recommend them for Apple/Mac IT support and training and WordPress and multimedia publishing.

*I dedicate **Sandcastle and Other Stories** to my parents. My mom was a terrific and inspiring artist, a lover of books, and a speed reader; along with giving me the idea for **Mothers of Twins**, she read some of these tales in very early form and gave good counsel . . . my dad was one of the most talented artists I've ever known, and a constant creative influence. He gave his blessing for this book, and I was humbled anew.*

WHAT OTHERS HAVE SAID ABOUT THE STORIES WITHIN THESE BOOK COVERS:

"Just read *The Virtue of Minding Your Own Business*. Oh my, what currents run deep! Beautifully seen, beautifully told. Praise praise praise ... Pardon my French, but you are one darn major American writer!

How can you never have been an actor in a monster suit? *Typecast* simply _jangles_ with been-there-done-that! I'll preliminarily believe you, but one day I'm gonna shout, 'ACTION!' when you're not looking and see if you don't grab a butcher knife and come ravening at the camera.

You do know that you have a wonderful fresh voice on the page, do you not?"

—Richard Bach, author of
Jonathan Livingston Seagull and **Illusions**

"Mr. Bog's characters range from contemptible wretches to disinterested observers; satisfied to watch life or death pass in front of them as they chronicle the tedium of life. We all know people like this, these are not the second stringers of life content to ride the bench, they are the third string, wallowing through life's torrents, drifting along, hoping that their seemingly erratic direction will steer them into safety and comfort. His characters stay close to the water, the beach or the river; looking for redemption, a cleansing, or a quick escape. In *Typecast* we meet a journeyman actor who falls all too easily into his character, a 'backwoods drug pusher and thief.'

In *When the Ship Sinks* the central character's total involvement consists of giving away the ending of a novel. 'The mortician did it,' he sulks as an interested party picks up a discarded book then tosses it away. In *Sandcastle* we listen in from an all too close perspective as an incredibly dark scene unfolds in front of us. It's the type of story that gives one nightmares; we're close to the tragedy, we try to scream and warn the victim but in this nightmare we've lost our voice so no one hears our scream. The waves crash, the ocean's warm water rushes over us but our voice is muted."

—John Malik, *The Huffington Post*

"This is a small collection of short stories that packs a large wallop. Unexpected, somewhat twisted, fantastical, but above all, poignant and extremely well written. **Sandcastle and Other Stories** announces the arrival of a thoughtful, accomplished talent from whom we will be hearing more in the future. A recommended read deserving of every one of the five stars I have to award it."

—Russell Blake, author of **Jet** and **Silver Justice**

"This is an excellent collection of stories, well written and compelling in their varied nature. The first story *The Virtue of Minding Your Own Business* is thought provoking, almost like a puzzle that needed to be pieced together so the full complexity of the story could be seen. Overall, the stories were constructed in a very literary style, which I really enjoyed. Great read. Highly recommend."

—Barry Crowther, author of **As the Sun Turns Black** and **Killing Flow**

"OMG! She just, her kid just, that lady just . . . that guy! Wow! Incredible story and such raw grit to the characters making them seem more real without overdramatics. Perfect dynamics flow of a family's longstanding argument. Superb!"

—Dianne "Dee" Solberg, author of **The Clysm Wars**, **The Bear Facts**, and runs the writing blog *ramble-inn.blogspot.com*, on *Sandcastle*

"Ooh, so good, I had to read it twice! The imagery is amazing, the characters brutal. Killer ending. Wow. Love it."

—Rachel Thompson, author of **A Walk in the Snark** and **The Mancode: Exposed**, on *Sandcastle*

"You have given me goosebumps! That was such a well-told story and the ending, well! I think I'm still in shock."

—Dionne Lister, author of **Shadows of the Realm**, on *Sandcastle*

"I knew I didn't like the beach for a reason. Amazing!"

—Jill Sundholm Pribilski, writer and creator of *jillcrazyquiltz.blogspot.com*, on *Sandcastle*

"Justin, you have the most wonderful imagination, and the painting from your dad is simply beautiful. Talent runs in abundance in the family, I see."

—Amberr Meadows, writer and creator of **Like a Bump on a Blog** at *amberrisme.com*, on *Sandcastle*

"Wow, this is a great story. Brutal, but very compelling."
—Elise Lufkin, from *sisterscook.blogspot.com*, on *Under the Third Story Window*

"Mmm... enjoyed the thoughts. Are those that think they are alone when sharing a time and space with others, not good listeners, or do they simply not ask the right questions along life's course?"
—David Freeman on *Train Crash*

"I was hooked (no pun intended) from the start. Superbly written!
—Katherine Meduna on *Poseidon Eyes*

"Wonderfully touching story . . . with beautiful writing, as always. One story anybody with siblings can relate to."
—Jane Isaac, author of **An Unfamiliar Murder**, on *Cats In Trees*

"This is brilliant. Really lovely to read and plays with the reader so expertly. I really wanted to read every word and I did, but couldn't work out precisely why. It's the characters I think. They're so 'show not told.' Thank you for this."
—Catherine Dreyer, a fellow writer and creator of *writeanovelin10minutesflat.wordpress.com*, on *Cats In Trees*

"This story is so beautiful, yet so melancholic and deeply sad . . . very good writing. And the cats are . . . like my daughter, Stuliana, says . . . very (Swiss cakes)."
—Stauroylla Papadopoulou, an early reader from Cyprus, on *Cats In Trees*

CONTENTS

Introduction 1

The Virtue of Minding Your Own Business 3
Sandcastle. 17
Mothers of Twins. 29
When the Ship Sinks. 65
Poseidon Eyes. 77
Cats In Trees. 105
Typecast 109
Under the Third Story Window. 131
On the Back Staircase 141
Train Crash. 161

BONUS: Chapter 1 from my first novel, the psychological family drama, Wake Me Up 171

Acknowledgements. 207
About the Author 211

INTRODUCTION

The first short story, *The Virtue of Minding Your Own Business*, was a runner-up in an Ernest Hemingway short story competition, and found publication in a journal alongside the winning entry. A tale of madness, murder, and regret . . . it is also the first of two stories inspired by the questionable thought: What if the only thing someone wanted to be was a tree? The other tree story here is titled *Cats In Trees*. As a whole, there are several tonal connections between the stories. Many have similar themes, often touching on a character's moment of darkness; twins are at play in three of the stories, *Mothers of Twins*, *The Virtue of Minding Your Own Business*, and *On the Back Staircase*—a highlight to the fact that I am a twin, and my younger siblings are also twins. *Sandcastle* and *When the Ship Sinks*, two stories where divorce is part of the central character's past, tackle this feeling of being unmoored from different perspectives. One story, *Poseidon Eyes*, perhaps set in an alternate fantasy world, received an honorable mention in **The Mississippi Review**, but was not published there. This story's twin or pairing is *Train Crash*, because the main characters can only see the world one way, and want so much to make something big happen. Finally, in the two stories, *Under the Third Story Window* and *Typecast*, I hoped to bring urgency to the situations using a raw tone. Throughout the collection I wanted to instill a slight sense of humor, a dry rush, and lend this to the characters. Please enjoy my very first short story collection. At the end there is a sneak peek, the opening chapter of my first novel, a psychological family drama, *Wake Me Up*. This novel will be published in 2013.

The Virtue of Minding Your Own Business

That's how I find Rachel, anyway, in the backyard of her father's vacation house on Maine Island, two miles offshore. One arm's up and alive, and the other's down and dead.

"Good day, Miss Rachel," I say, just in passing, getting about my morning chores. She, of course, doesn't respond, but her eyes do, and that's enough for me.

I'm the head gardener for Mr. Barrons, Jr. Usually I don't feel awkward around Rachel Barrons, his daughter. She likes to watch me plant tomatoes near the back fence and she makes sure I give all the myrtle and alyssum enough water, and drench the begonias. I started them in scattered patches circling the oaks. By the end of summer season, Labor Day weekend, they should be puffy and vibrant green, white, deep pink and purple blossoms. When I work the annuals, the perennials, or the new trees into the soil, Rachel always has a half smile on her face, sort of hiding something almost, as if she might break if she showed too much. But she never gives me any trouble, doesn't get in my way or waste my time yapping at me like Vicki Calmagalli, Rachel's maid, does whenever I pass close by the estate house to do the trimming along the front hedges. I have an assistant now, Russ Darnton, who I ordinarily send to do the close housework, but I like to keep my hand in, let the owner know I've still got my faculties.

Rachel stays statuesque in the backyard almost an hour later, and to an outsider, would possibly appear to be practicing some form of artistic dance. Her slim frame bends at the waist as if in slow motion, something I call tree time, while her legs remain ramrod straight together with her feet splayed. Her movements change from moment to moment, her upper body contorting into a twist at the waist, and her arms swinging upwards, reaching for the light of the afternoon sun. Sometimes she stays rooted in the same position for hours. Vicki comes out with food for her: apples and nuts and other fruits from trees.

"You've got to drink now." I hear Vicki's tone, a put upon thing, as if she never expected to be following this girl around the island, making her do basic things. I don't see how it takes much out of Vicki's day, but some people love to vent more than most.

The only thing Rachel drinks is water, and it's like she won't ever stop drinking from the plastic container Vicki hands her, but she does, lets it drop from her grasp, and then stares off towards the bay. Vicki picks up the water bottle from the grass, letting out a displeased grunt, and heads back to the estate house, where she can start making a list of food to get on the mainland.

The story starts and ends with Rachel, and there's a lot of junk left over, slivering its way into the mess. She's my muse; I like to think of her that way; I'm a gardener who wants to come to terms; I'm a collector of information, and I write everything down. I've kept a journal since I was a boy at the Little Red Schoolhouse on Conway Road, across the water and in the country five miles. I won't say I'm grammatically correct either; the words get written even if you think you know how to use them without a diploma. Three years ago the schoolhouse was made an historic site, with old photographs of the teachers and the children wearing knickers and sturdy shoes, winter boots and heavy wool coats stitched by hand. I'm in one of the pictures, small and curious, looking at the flashbulb, the brightness bringing me into the newness of the event, a moth to flame; on one side of me sits my twin brother, Edgar, the mirror image of us split down the middle of a rotten apple core. Sitting on the other side of me was one of the Dobbs' girls, both girls dead now long years of cancer in their middle ages. We were placed on a row of benches, with the tall people in the upper grades standing like lighthouses behind us.

I had the urge to learn more than any kid in the whole district, but one thing can hold a child back, and only one thing. It still does, and that's money. It can rule the world, and up in the wild of Maine in the early twenties, it ruled my world. I was even planning on running away once, to find a way of my own. Now, money, I've come to realize, haunts people. Take Rachel, for example. She's a young woman, with all this modern technology available, who should be able to do anything she pleases, should be able to make her own way in the world, but the money twisted her as tree roots under sidewalks tend to make the concrete buckle, made her world crack with pressure. I saw it all.

I became a handyman, and started my own lawn service for the wealthy flocking to Maine Island, the summer people who didn't listen to so much local gossip. After the depression, two years after I was released from school at sixteen, after my mother died of pneumonia in thirty-eight, after Edgar was put in the prison up in Lightfoot, I made a connection with a man named Barrons—he owned half the island.

While wringing my best hat, tighter, I told Mr. Barrons what I could do for his property: I could build a fence that would last his lifetime, plant a tree to watch the world grow in, and I soon became his personal property, an honest, diligent, close-tongued worker. I've been here ever since, and never went back to school though the urge still is with me even at the age of seventy-three. When I die, all my journals, notebooks about the island, the differences from year to year, the bird migrations, May snowfalls, winter blizzards, shipwrecks on the rocks off Vivian's Point, will be packed off to the historical society over in Barton. I was born there in a small office in back of the police station, the only place the town doctor, Mr. Hawthorne, who was really only part real doctor and part animal vet, could get to, the only place that was open during the worst storm of 1919. I want people to read what I write, but there are some personal things I'll have to rip out and burn, cast into the wind with me.

Rachel Barrons wants to be a tree. I've watched her grow.

It's as simple a diagnosis as that, and I don't need a psychology degree to tell you that. She's always loved the outdoors since she was a kid when she helped me plant a patch of dogwoods and several of the apple trees bordering the brambles and deadfall forest making up most of the island. The dogwoods touch the sky now.

Mr. Barrons, Jr. only comes out here for the month of August, and leaves soon after Labor Day. His father gave me my start, and

Mr. Barrons, Jr. takes after him. He kept me on and expects me to act like nothing's changed. When a man dies, a friend of mine, someone who treated me with respect, one of the few on this mortal plane, a piece of me would fly away. I never thought I'd go back to the island after Mr. Barrons died.

I stayed on the mainland for a year, hooked up with Carrolson Lawn Service over at the Country Club. Mr. Barrons, Jr. let the island go to weeds that summer. He kept the place locked up the whole year. It was his right; he was mourning. The people who lived on the other half of Maine Island tried to do something special, to let the Barrons' family know how they felt; they were behind him and respected him. They offered to have his lot landscaped by a different company. The Potters, the Jarvis's, the Dunlops, and the Van Burens all pitched in and beautified the island, Mr. Barrons' property, without me, and without my input, even though I'd taken care of the place for decades.

And it isn't any secret that I was seen as a drifter, even after so much water under the bridge, someone from the mainland who couldn't be trusted. No one forgot about my brother, Edgar, for a good while after that, dry times for me, until Mr. Barrons, Jr. came back the next year, walked into the Country Club (where I had begged to be a step-and-fetch-it) and asked me if I wanted to continue working on his estate. He said, "It's what Father would've liked."

I quit and made my residence in a little place on the island Mr. Barrons, Jr. set me up in. It was the old servants' quarters near the deadened field littered with large boulders facing Marker Bay. It had one room, a small waist-high refrigerator, a burner, and a bathroom with a shower: all I ever needed. I moved out of my father's house and I've lived on the island ever since. My father and I didn't miss each other. Edgar followed me around. He was my shadow, my twin who was darker than the beach in November when the moon is lost behind gray clouds, and the wind rips the swells up into shooting blankets of ice and spray along the coast. When they locked Edgar away, I wrote in my journal that they almost locked me up with him, as if we'd been joined at the hip. We looked alike, identical twins, but we grew apart from birth. He wasn't satisfied with earning a living, only believed in taking, felt that youth is deserving of anything the old have, as if by right. Anything I had, even if he couldn't use it, he took. When he took Mary Norbertson, someone saw him, and they came after him and found me. Simple.

I was locked up immediately. I'll never forget the jail and the old stench of urine in the back corner of the county cell. I told them it wasn't me, but they didn't listen. They wanted me to tell them where she was, where I disposed of the body. I didn't have any alibi. Father was in Bridgeport, no one was home when my brother took Mary, pulled her into Ferris State Woods, and forced her to do what he wanted, rape, murder, crimes you read about in the pulp mysteries, happening in the cities, down in Bangor and beyond. They couldn't find the body. Mary went missing for the next couple days. Edgar hid in the woods while I was treated to hell week in the Maine prison system. Mary's parents came in and tried to kill me. Mr. Norbertson pulled a gun out and shouted at me to tell him where she was. I backed into the pissed-out corner, my hands scraping the wall behind me, and pleaded with him. It wasn't me. It wasn't me. It had to be my brother. I told them I love Mary. Mrs. Norbertson forced her husband's arm down. She did it calmly, resolutely, and sadly, accusingly, with a face void of everything but understanding. She moved gracefully, as if under water, slow, and I'll never forget that.

They caught Edgar the next day and let me out even though most of them thought we both were in on the crime together; I was the mastermind because I was more intelligent—imagine them calling a stupid man like me intelligent. After that, I hid within myself. Mr. Barrons rescued me. They found Mary, her corpse, near one of Bear Creek's two-foot waterfalls, under a twist of vines. Edgar was put away; he died in the state penitentiary at the age of sixty-two, a lifer. I never visited him. How could I? I don't think anyone in our family did. Mother was put to rest a long time ago and Father was a man who hadn't learned, with so much hardship, how to forgive. I took after him in my own ways. He couldn't bear to see much of me either. I was a reminder of a life, a person, he wanted cut off forever. Often I became, felt like, a murderer myself in my father's presence. When Mr. Barrons, Jr. came to me I jumped at the idea of moving out, away from my father, and setting up a new life on the island I had come to think of as my own.

My father died a year later, all alone and so bitter that the pain he felt eating within him after his wife, his son, me, the doppelgänger, left him, was too much to contemplate day after day; he withered to the bone and drifted out of this world. His funeral gathered a small group of people over at Barton Town Cemetery. He was placed next to my mother. After I moved out he sold the two plots in front of his, the ones that had been reserved for Edgar and me. I don't even know where Edgar is buried, I didn't want to find out more when the letter arrived, but I wonder if there's a Lifer Cemetery on all prison grounds and who visits or sends flowers to wither and die on all those criminal graves.

And this all gets back to Rachel because just looking at her out in the back hollow of oaks and hemlock trees, the sound of the waves crashing along the shore an eighth of a mile beyond, conjures up images from the past. I can't help it. I try to be as nice and natural with Rachel as possible. I can't help feeling drawn to her, sorry for her.

Sometimes she takes her thinking too far. If she believes she's alone, Rachel will bring her tan arms up over her head so they point to the sky, fingers outstretched to capture the breadth. Many times, as I grasp the long wooden handles of my shears and cut the hedge lining the back patio, I've watched her grab her long dusty blonde hair and pull it high to hang from her fingers.

I never married all these years working the earth. I think I used up too much to share with anyone else. Vicki tells anyone she pleases all about my past, lets all who are interested in passing the time know more about my twin brother than even I did, how tragic my whole existence is, that I should be pitied. I don't correct her to let her know her backdoor wisdom yanks me deep into another country, where water runs uphill. I'm just glad she doesn't really know anything about me. She doesn't know I had one great love, one wonderful yearning, and the satisfaction, although destroyed, more than enough to last double my lifetime. I've become a fixture on the island, and I won't retire until I can't make sense of my own fingers in front of me, how they open and how they close. When I die, I have specific instructions left in my small apartment, written on one of those new holographic wills. My ashes will be spread in the water off the coast, between the island and the mainland, which, I believe, will set me free.

Today, Rachel surprises me.

Without my expecting it, she screams at the dying birches in the yard, "Look at me. I'm a majestic willow. Stay alive." Whenever she yells out like that I jump a little, as if I was just cold-goosed, putter around a bit with no direction, and then continue on track with the trimming and weeding.

Probably caught up in her own world, imagining how selfish she's being to the birches, because she's not diseased, is very vital, and a willow with pride, Rachel will drop her hair down, twist it into a ball behind her and frown. Maybe she wants to let the birches know she understands how they're feeling: the life running out of them. She'll usually stand next to her favorite birch, one that still has real color in its branches, a little green at the edges around the white, no haphazard scabs of chalky bark peeling horribly down its side. Then she'll stretch her right arm up in front of her and press her left arm tight to her side because one of the tree's main branches had been torn off in a thunderstorm last September. Where the branch used to be is an open, blackening hole. She'll cry then and I always want to help someone who's crying; it's in my nature.

I want her to notice me today so I can cheer her up—catch her eyes, find a coloring lucidity. Her left arm's been up in the air now for over an hour, and she must ache. I say, "Hello, Rachel, perfect day," as I balance myself on my heels for a second and then stuff my hands into my front pockets because I don't know what to do with them. I can never remain motionless for long, stand still without fiddling with my hands. Rachel blinks her watery blue eyes as if she's coming out of hibernation.

"Oh," is all she says back to me, but she then loosens her outstretched arm and comes away from whatever she was doing, whatever place she kept company.

"I was planning on boating into town if you want to come along," I say. Even though I know the answer will be no, I like to be polite and include Rachel in all of my island courtesy. It's not the first time I've asked Rachel how she's doing, carried on small talk, and I hope it won't be the last. I've been on this island so long I like to feel I set an example to all the new people, those who fall in love with the beauty of the isolation, the water, and the serenity of Maine Island. The town boat only leaves for the mainland three times a day. I use her father's Chris Craft to get supplies whenever I want. It's a good, strong boat and it's a beautiful day: calm blue, mild waves that don't cover up the dangerous rocks you can run your boat on near shore. I'm just being polite.

"No. I think I'll stay here and look at all the trees."

"Well, just thought I'd ask." I'm happy just getting a response; there's a spark of light inside my stomach. I walk forward and peer closely at one of the dying birches, and say, "Going to have to cut down these diseased trees sometime." Rachel's face becomes pale even in the hot, bright summer sun. I don't know what's wrong with her. I do know she's here to recover in some way from some illness she had, and Mr. Barrons, Jr. told me not to upset his Rachel, told me to stay away from her, but I'm always friendly; don't see the harm in a little chit chat, a friend would do that, heck, an acquaintance would too—just look at that dreadful maid of Rachel's, Vicky Calmagalli, always looking both directions of suspicion wherever I walk; I've heard her say worse.

Rachel quickly wraps her arms around a dead thin-trunk birch the color of burnt egg whites, and won't budge. She stays that way for hours. Mr. Barrons, Jr. can't put sense into her. He keeps eyeing me and asking me what exactly did I say to her because Rachel stays silent and won't talk no matter how much her father pleads.

If I could go back in time, I'd try to warn Mary Norbertson away from my brother and away from me. She looked so beautiful. I can picture her standing in front of her farm the first time I saw her, feeding a small group of hens, just starting the day, glancing at me and Edgar as we passed on our way to school. In two years, she'd be wrapped in twisting vines, but back then I'd get to know her better; I'd take her on long walks along the shore road, and talk to her about where she wanted to go after I got out of school; I'd promised to take her away. I'll always remember her stare and the fullness of her hair as I ran my fingers through it. The first couple days Edgar and I passed her farm she always gave us curious looks, as if watching identical boys gave her pleasure. She was trying to find the differences between us. I always dream how Edgar walked nearer to her, his every step hiding cracked energy. Mary stood out in the yard like Rachel stands now. Time passed and Mary sensed the difference, the danger, that it wasn't me this time, coming to force her away, change her life. It seemed destined, and such a waste. In my dreams I can help Mary. Instead of Edgar slinking towards her, I replace him, and bow to her when she smiles without any fear. I take her hand, lead her back to the farmhouse, tell her I'm sorry, and that I'll always love you. Go inside, I say, and she does. When Edgar arrives in the early evening I jump out of the shadows and tell him to choose his future; I tell him to let his pain go, that I never wanted Mary. Everything I had, he took away from me. In my dream, I tell him he doesn't want to take Mary, and I offer myself instead. Mary's image flies away and Rachel replaces her: broken and pained, standing on the lawn like the woman who haunts my dreams.

All night Rachel clings to the tree, and that's the last image I have of her before I go back to my little place at the far end of the island. No one wanted me around—a feeling I was always aware of, picked up quick. When I come to help Russ mow the backyard the next afternoon, Vicki strolls out as if she was waiting all day to tell me, throw her bitter barbs with born relish, Rachel left on the morning boat, has gone back to whatever place Mr. Barrons, Jr. keeps her.

"I don't know what you said, and I'm not telling on you, but you got no business giving Miss Rachel such a fright, old man." Whenever Vicki says she's not doing something, I believe the opposite.

"Your feet hurting today, Vicki?"

"Don't you never you mind my feet," she says with emphasis on that last word. She turns her back just as slowly, as if she hasn't a care in the world, and shuts the door behind her. My mother, so long ago now—I can picture her heart-shaped face as if she stood right in front of me at that very moment—always said that people in pain, the meanest, the most bitter, must have sore feet. Vicki should soak her feet in an Epsom Salt bath every black night.

I can't help but notice the dead birch tree Rachel's arms wrapped around so fiercely yesterday is now gone, roots, stump, and all. What remains is a dark hole I'll have to fill in with new dirt and patch with sod, and I want to rap on the door and ask Vicki what is really wrong with Rachel, but bite my tongue. She'd be more than happy to fill me in. For once, I keep my questions to myself, push Mary's image away to that place inside where it bubbles below the surface and start the lawnmower on the second try.

Sandcastle

Brenda watched the orange balloon float into the air above the beach. Dipping and circling in the hot breeze, it reminded her of the time her ex-husband had filled her bedroom with three hundred balloons to surprise her on their first anniversary. She was very glad she'd never have to see him, the brutish shit, again. Four years gone, wasted, her married years had been as predictable as her parents told her they would be. Sometimes she imagined her parents were part of an ancient coven, where her future mistakes were played with like bitter fortunes tossed into a black cauldron.

Jumping up and down, tugging at her mother's hand, Jane, a little girl in a tutu-styled bathing suit, started to whine.

"I want another balloon." Jane's mother in the turquoise bikini flicked the girl's hand away.

"No, Jane. Go play in the water. Danny Richards is down there. Do you see him? Go play with him. I have to rest. And don't bother me. You mind Danny's mother." The girl's mother sighed, wondered if the people lounging close to her on the crowded beach could hear her, picked up a bottle next to her and slathered sunscreen all over the little girls arms, shoulders, face; she then put her adult-sized hands firmly on the little girl's shoulders and said, "If I'm not here, if I've gone to the restrooms, what do you do?" The girl couldn't squirm out of her mother's grasp. "Stay with Danny." The girl's mother glanced over at a concave-bellied boy, a toddler very much the same age as her child, twenty yards away, closer to the waves rolling in, and spotted a woman in a ridiculous white-feathered one-piece swimsuit. She waved to this woman, a polite wave to someone you know but don't want to know well.

From a beach towel space away, Brenda took the scene in. The beach was crowded, but the background noise didn't bother her at all; Brenda believed she could hide in a crowd, and wondered why being alone was something she deserved. She found herself enjoying the discomfort in the mother and daughter's close conversation; she almost laughed out loud when Jane's mouth opened like an outstretched bow. The kid deserves what she gets, Brenda thought. She tilted her head away to make it look like she wasn't paying attention, but only just slightly. She saw everything.

"But . . . I want my balloon."

Brenda, her pistachio-colored beach chair squeaking when she moved slightly, noticed a string of saliva dribble from Jane's mouth and down her chin. Jane's mother pushed her octagon-shaped sunglasses into the hair above her forehead and stared, her eyes somehow cold and reflecting nothing, at her daughter. "What did I just say to you, Jane? Forget the goddamn balloon. I told you I didn't want to buy it for you . . . you're blocking my sun. If you don't leave me alone and go play, you'll find yourself at home right now. Be a big little girl for Mommy. If you can do this, I promise I'll give you another swimming lesson later. Your dog paddle is coming along fine. Go play."

Brenda tried to smile, but couldn't, as she thought about her life and what it would've been like if her baby had lived, would this new presence in her family be capable of healing a prickling rift under her heels, make her husband's boots stop flailing about—always making contact by accident, didn't mean to do that, you know me, you know me, you know me. Her life could be broken down into a twisted children's rhyme. Right, Brenda, first comes love, then comes marriage; then comes miscarriage, and her goals and planning stopped there. She hated the simple way her life unfolded and the way it seemed so goddamn planned. Ever since she was little she'd been under someone else's control. When she was twenty, almost two years away from graduation at the community college, she met Jake and they moved in together. Brenda's parents never trusted Jake; they could tell the first second they spotted him hoisting himself off his motorcycle, then slicking back his sun-bleached hair and finally tugging at the devil-pointed goatee that he was just putting on a big show (her father's words). They wouldn't speak to her for months until her twenty-first birthday when they relented and finally knew Jake would, for better or worse, be a part of their daughter's future. They stopped asking Brenda if she was going to finish college. All they could do was warn her when Jake wasn't around, try to undermine what was happening all along. "Is he hitting you again, Brenda?" her mother would whisper to her when Jake and Father were in the living room watching the Sunday football extravaganza, neither of them speaking to the other, just grunting from their Lazyboys, the kind with the built-in beer holders on the arms. All her parents could do was watch and say "I told you so" later, which they did all the time.

How could Brenda reply? Her control had shifted territory, from one of family questionings and buttonholes, to the scary realm of Jekyll and Hyde. It was one thing she wanted to handle alone, without her parents' interference. Jake was the sweetest man she had ever met, at first, before the wedding, and wouldn't even lay a finger on her neck to caress her. It started after the wedding when he slapped her on the butt too hard, a prelude to lovemaking he said, and when she complained, he hit her harder. Of course, he always tried to make it up to her afterwards. He took her to movies she wanted to see, to the roadhouses for drinks, and took her shopping, but never at the good stores, just the second hand malls where he worked in rotation as a night security guard.

Another thing Brenda hated was the way she often caught her mother scrutinizing her. Her mother's chin wrinkled up, and her eyes opened just almost all the way and sly, as if her mother had foreseen Brenda's downfall, as if she was used goods now and any other man could smell Jake's lousy scent all over her and she would never hear the sound of grandchildren. She said to Brenda, with her patented matter-of-fact tightness, "A lot of women have miscarriages. And a lot of women, today anyway, fail at meeting the right man." What her mother didn't have to say was "How dare you do this to our family;" the tone of her voice was enough. At times, Brenda liked to picture her parents, naked, with witch paint splashed across their bodies, dancing around an effigy of Brenda. In her daydream, she would force the effigy to come to life and make it bash her parents' heads together to let them know they were not always right.

Their spoken predictions of failure had started when she brought her fiancé home for the first time, when Brenda was helping her mother cut salad cucumbers and rip iceberg lettuce, when her mother, in a voice of thinly veiled anger, asked her how long she'd known Jake and asked her if she was really serious about ruining her life with a man like that. Now, her mother gives her books on how to choose your mate and her father still curses her former husband at the dinner table, even though it's been years since the divorce. He looks at Brenda and chuckles, wiser in hindsight, and says he told her not to marry the bastard.

Brenda watched as Jane ran into the water and yelled something to a boy named Danny Richards. She didn't know whether Jane's mother would've actually taken the girl home, but it did seem as if Jane didn't want to stick around and find out. I wouldn't even bring the whiny girl, Brenda thought, which made her remember her own lost child, the image of a dashed possibility always close to the surface, and Brenda frowned even more because she knew she was a liar. There was a time in her marriage when she fervently believed this surprise baby could've saved her, and that her husband could've changed if he only held a tiny baby in his arms, focused on something good and pure for once—she knew this was a ridiculous thought. If her baby had lived she would've taken her everywhere and she'd never send her away with an imperious flick of the wrist.

The mother readjusted her sunglasses on her nose and then lowered her bikini top an inch, giving anyone trudging by in the sand a tantalizing view. Brenda envied the woman's body. It was what her magazines called sumptuous and glandularly flawless. She started comparing her thirty-year-old, freckled, oblong body to that of Jane's mother's perfect figure.

She's had a kid, is a kid herself, and she still looks like Miss America, Brenda thought. I've had a miscarriage, gained twenty pounds, which I can't seem to lose, failed in marriage, even though it wasn't all my fault, and I still live with my parents, who remind me nearly every chance they get about the chronological order of every wrong turn I took.

Brenda jumped when a sea gull landed barely a foot away from her hand, wings expanding and then closing as tight as cabbage leaves, and dug its beak into a Snickers' wrapper. She picked up *Gone With The Wind*, brushed the sand off the cover, and wondered what it would be like to be Scarlett O'Hara. Before she opened to her place, the fiery tension-filled scene where Atlanta was about to burn, Brenda pulled down the top of her blue one-piece an inch, but gave up when even that one inch uncovered her tiny beige nipples.

After letting out a short sigh, Brenda started to read. The sea gull flew into the air with a jerk and landed a few feet farther away where a discarded Popsicle stick stuck out of the sand like some ancient totem pole carved to appease the god of sand fleas.

A bronzed man wearing a string of cloth that barely passed for a bathing suit and barely covered his privates paused between Jane's mother and Brenda and stood staring at the choppy blue surf. He sucked in his breath, showing striated stomach and chest muscles. Brenda lowered her book a few inches and watched the man tilt his head her way. Her right hand fluttered around her neck. She involuntarily dropped the book on the sand beside her. The man turned towards Jane's mother, sat down next to her hot-pink towel, adjusted what hid within his bathing suit with a pass of his hand and stared at what must be high impact aerobics-toned legs. Brenda's fluttering hand started to claw into the soft flesh of her neck below the chin.

"Haven't seen you here before." The man stretched out a weightlifter's arm. "My name's Carver." Jane's mother shook his hand lightly and took off her sunglasses.

"I'm Patricia. But you can call me Trish." Brenda almost choked when she heard the innocent, playful tone of the woman's voice. Her face turned red when she saw the man motion towards the water with an eye glance, caught how Trish slyly peeled off her wedding band and secreted it away in her purse, watched as he blocked Jane's mother's sun, witnessed how he took her hand and then strolled with her down to the water's edge. The gull, the totem pole in its beak, flew away to the boardwalk.

Too busy building a sandcastle with Danny Richards, Jane didn't notice her mother enter or exit the water twenty feet away.

Carver and Trish flung themselves down on the beach towel like two glistening seals about to sun themselves on territorial rocks. They made small talk in whispers Brenda couldn't hear. She tried to concentrate on her favorite novel, on the story she reread every couple of years, on the rebel inside Scarlett and the man who wanted to tame her, but threw the thick trade paperback down and vowed never to read another book that portrayed a woman as some object made for a righteous man.

Brenda's envy grew as Carver rubbed oil onto Trish's shoulders. Their voices became louder over the course of their game play.

"So," Jane's mother said, "when did you plan on leaving? You could use some cool shade." She emphasized the last two words by trailing her fingers along his thigh, down to his knee. Brenda tipped her head back to make it look like she was sleeping behind her rose-tinted sunglasses, but she kept an eye on the man and the woman.

Jake, her ex-husband, had never come to the beach with Brenda, would've never been caught dead wearing what Carver wore for fear of being ridiculed, but she would've liked him to be there right now. Brenda's old husband was over six-two and weighed more than a small car, and he had turned mean and sour and drinking buddies asked him if he had ever appeared in those biker movies. She would've told her former husband that the muscle man had called him a freak, a cupcake, and the woman had laughed at him and whispered that the cupcake's MOTHER tattoo was probably spelled M-U-D-D-A. Brenda knew her former husband, if pushed just right, could be brutal, and divorced him for that very reason after weeks of counseling at a women's shelter, but he'd come in handy right now.

"Oh, I don't know," said Carver. "How about you?"

Trish glanced at her watch. "Well, I've got close to an hour free right now, and I do need shade—badly."

As the two stood up, Jane's mother turned towards the parking lot, started walking and stopped when Carver said, "Don't you want to take your things?"

"No. I'll get them afterwards. Let's make this hour last." Her voice sounded cold, distant, for a moment, as if she couldn't wait to get back to the beach, but only for an instant. Carver led her to his car and drove to his beach house a mile away. Brenda had heard him tell Trish about his wonderful secluded house with blackout curtains in the master bedroom, and Brenda watched them leave; their every step across the burning sand and congested boardwalk.

Jane said, "I want to build a sandcastle with a moat." Danny said, "I don't want any water around my castle." Jane started whining, and then they grabbed the towers they had already formed with their pails and flung fistful after fistful of wet sand at each other.

Crying, with sand in her eyes, sand in her mouth, sand down her tutu, Jane ran back to her mother's towel in search of what Brenda knew was comfort and understanding and someone Jane could tattle her story to. Brenda saw how beautiful the girl would be when she was grown up, how manipulative and clever the girl's vocabulary would become with topflight, private schooling, how carefree the girl's life would be with no one around her harping at her for being stupid and ruining her future by making mistakes of the heart; Jane would be the one in control. Like mother, like daughter.

Jane's crying stopped as she searched for her mother, but Brenda could tell she was ready to turn the tears back on again in a second. Jane glanced Brenda's way, and Brenda smiled so widely, so friendly, that Jane ran up to her, still pinching sand out of her suit.

"Have you seen my mother?"

Everything came together for Brenda at that moment. Her father could curse all he wanted to, but the next time he laughed smugly at the dinner table, flaunting his superiority while staring at Brenda, she'd spit in his face. She'd race away from the table, gather all the How-To books her mother gave her, dump them in the kitchen sink, burn them up and then start the disposal.

Brenda pulled her sunglasses off, stood up beside Jane and pointed at a swimmer out near the deep water and the buoys with the undertow warnings.

"You're Jane?" The girl nodded her head. "Your mother left me a message for you. Don't you see her swimming out there?" All Jane could see was reflected sun on choppy water, little slick-headed people jumping closer to shore and a brown-haired head bobbing through the rolling ocean waves far in the distance. She squinted her eyes down to slits.

"Yes," Jane said hesitantly.

"She asked me to tell you to swim out to her."

Jane's eyes blinked in the sun. "But I can't swim that good yet."

"She told me to tell you that she would give you that swimming lesson you wanted earlier once you reached her." Brenda spoke every word slowly and watched the muscles in the girl's legs twitch as she shifted from one foot to the other in the hot sand. "Have you ever heard of the little engine who kept saying, 'I think I can. I think I can?'"

"Sure I have."

"Well, your mother thinks you're a good enough swimmer now. She told me so and we both had fun watching you splash around in the shallow water with Danny. I think your dog paddle is good enough also and your mother will be very proud of you.

You go on. I'll wave to her and let her know you're coming. She'll meet you halfway, in the shallow part."

"Will you watch me too?"

"Of course, Jane."

Jane said thanks gleefully and raced for the water.

When she was a good thirty feet offshore she turned back. Brenda waved at her and pointed off to the girl's left. Jane turned in that direction and resumed her slow dog paddling.

After watching a whitecap dunk the girl, Brenda gathered up her chair and her bag, but left her novel half-buried in the sand. She waited on the beach until the waves blocked her view.

Mothers of Twins

I remember the day perfectly when Connie Yonker, President of the Southern Michigan Mothers of Twins Club, waltzed into my hospital room as spunky as Ginger Rogers in an old movie musical. I gave birth to a set of twin boys only ten hours before, and it rained heavily outside my window, April showers, keeping the current Michigan spring gloom at bay. The humidity from the steam outside was barely held in check by the ancient heating and cooling system. In late April there's always so much rain, a dispassionate sheet of gray and a stretch of overcast days to get the tulips blooming. 24 hours before I gave birth I told Jack, my husband, I didn't want to deliver in the rain, but I guess I didn't have a choice. It's funny sometimes when I think about how many days it can rain without a break, when the waters rise along the river running through town and push over the banks to flood Maple Street. When that happens no one can get through to the local grocery store for bread or frozen dinners.

Under my thin hospital blanket, with gentle circles, I rubbed the area around the bandaged sutures spread across my belly; I wanted some relief when, tap-tap on the unlatched door, Connie knocked like a woodpecker high from the aroma given off by her giant Gucci handbag, and burst into my room. A very tan, very thin small woman in a Day-Glo-yellow rain slicker smiled with such obvious guile; her red skirt peeked out under the coat lining, and her sleeves were rolled up almost to her elbows. Her eyes were big and I swear they almost glowed in vibrant aqua. I stayed silent for a moment just staring into those irises of hers because of the unreal and distracting quality; a sparkling alien-like feeling washed over me and in my mind it felt like the rain. She held her big purse loosely and it swung down near her knees.

She came right up to my bedside and stuck out her hand, which appeared fragile, tiny, with tan veins crossing along the back and gold rings with emerald green and diamonds on two of her fingers. "Hel-lo," she said, and the cheer and welcoming she put into her voice startled me, made me think of the voices telephone solicitors use when you first respond to them with a puzzled tone, when it's too late and they have you in their verbal trap.

"You look marvelous now don't you?" she added, the last word tilting upward. "The radiance of a new mother of twins! I must say: Wow!"

I didn't immediately know what to say but I certainly knew I did not look as good as this woman said I looked. Since the birth was cesarean and my abdominal and uterine walls were cut up, the doctor told me my stomach and everywhere would bloat even more until the gas could be released. Now I had to read up online about the current C-Section recovery tips, another thing to add to my ever-growing list of mommy chores (maybe Jack could handle this one, research it all at home, find out what the doctors aren't telling us, place me into a paranoid papoose, and I know he means well, but it's still very hard for me to actually do what he tells me to do, so maybe not—the deranged pre-birth mommy thoughts filling my head as I confronted this strange woman in front of me). They had told me ten hours into labor that natural birth, the event Jack and I had practiced once a week and on our own after class, would damage one of the boys because of his position. I was still getting bigger and bigger, my skin color tinged a sickly yellow—and maybe that's what she confused me with: the radiance of a human lemon. I felt unclean after having only one sponge bath since the delivery. All I wanted was an explanation for the strange intrusion so I kept quiet and waited for the woman to go on speaking.

Because my arms were under the blanket and I didn't bring them out to shake hands, her fingers jittered a little dance in the air before lowering. She winked like a mime telling me she understood my weakness, my rudeness. "Well, I do say you look splendid after giving birth to twin boys." Again, she spoke the last word louder than the rest, as if she'd been a cheerleader in her younger days and the habit never dissipated; I finally asked her who she was.

"Connie Yonker, of East Point. You know—the small subdivision past Adams Road, near Cranbrook, the one next to Christian Hills. I'm in charge of all recruiting in this region; I've been President of the Mothers of Twins Club for going on almost ten years this June." She let that sink in.

I thought she worked fast. Who was her connection at the hospital? Who was the person on the Labor and Delivery staff who informed this—I was growing ever-so-prickly now in my discomfort—cheery woman of all the twin births at St. Lukes Hospital. Wasn't it against the law to divulge patient information? I certainly thought so and for a second I was on the verge of really getting angry. I breathed deeply two times, counting to ten in my head, with sound effects and made myself calm again. If I started shouting I didn't want this happy woman to tell me I wasn't feeling well because of bad postpartum feelings. I felt the awkwardness in the air and Connie brightly persevered through my darkening mood.

"Right now I'm very tired," I said, and before I could get out another word she broke in and told me that was only natural and she'd only take another minute of my time and wasn't it an awful day to be stuck in a hospital with the rain and all.

"When I gave birth to my first set of twins I think it was hailing pellets as big as chick peas. So I know what it's like."

"You've had two sets of twins?" I couldn't believe a woman so trim could have any kid at all. I wondered if she felt superior about being able to bounce right back into shape—if she ever revealed this secret pride. My own mother remained a little heavy, twenty pounds or so, after having my brother and me, but we weren't twins; forevermore, three years apart, Chad would always be my older brother. I know my mother was thin at one time because of photographs my father took before they got married, when he courted her, gave up his big man on campus cad ways, when he asked her to pose and be enigmatic, like Elizabeth Taylor, my mother's favorite celebrity back in the sixties. She still is beautiful, but I wonder if I take after her because we do have similar body types.

"Oh yes, and my first pregnancy was a single girl. I have five children. All girls. The youngest finished up two years past at the

M-S-U in K-Zoo. I've got an empty nest to fill, wistfully." Who says wistfully out loud? Now I know. I'd been wondering who actually speaks like Connie in the real world, outside of books and films and she's alone on an island. She sat down in the brown vinyl chair three feet away from the bed without a thought and flipped her hair back, which was a damp sand color still eking out a last drop of rain water at the ends. And, I thought, plenty of time to fill now.

"Amazing," I muttered. I think it gave Connie some satisfaction because she heard me, and her smile widened a fraction even though there was something wrong with it. It wasn't a happy smile and again I wondered why she was here at all. I wasn't as weary as I thought and I very much wanted to see my baby boys again. The nurse said they had to have a battery of tests to make sure they were functioning right but it wouldn't be long until they were back; Jack would be here soon when he got off work. I wanted him here all day, but we had a major design account and the work had to be done. My want wasn't a need.

I guess it's instinctive to want to show off your children. This woman of twins, Connie Yonker from East Point, probably had a purse full of baby photos. On second thought, I didn't want her to see my children because I'd always know that she felt my children, anyone's children, couldn't measure up to hers. Then I scolded myself because I knew that was natural of any mother.

"Like they say: it's painful no matter the number you have. You've just experienced the most incredible moment of your life and you *do* positively glow." Her hands came together and she rocked back and forth slightly as if to confirm her words. She didn't even know me, yet she spoke to me as if we were old college roommates reunited after decades. The room filled with her perfume; the light scent of lavender mixed with the ever-present industrial cleaning detergent and medicinal rubbing alcohol.

What could make a woman say such a thing to a complete stranger? This whole scene reminded me of the time Jack and I met a German woman named Sunke who thought all Americans were superficial, just pretending to be nice when really they could care less. We met Sunke in Munich on our honeymoon while sitting all afternoon in an English Garden Seehaus with mass steins of beer littering the table. She had stop-sign-red hair, which was the *in* thing at the time over there after that Run Lola film, and she sat down close to us, the expression on her face a thin line, German, tight on a sunny lazy day. After listening to us for a bit, she joined our conversation. It was fun trying to understand her English. Strangely, she had a Scottish accent when she spoke English. She could converse fairly well, said she loved practicing her English.

I asked her what she thought of America and Americans and she scoffed and said we were always pretending to be nice, what is the word, she said, "Such a superficial people. When you go to a restaurant," she spoke in slow cadence, trying to find the right phrase, "in the United States, the waitress are nice to you. Don't even know you and they are nice to you. I think they are very fake."

Jack wanted to tell her that if the German waitresses and waiters had a tip incentive they'd be nice too, and that we'd get faster and better service also, but he didn't because he thought her talk was different and it was nice to learn something from a culture even if it was one of our petty faults. When we asked her if she'd been to America she said no and we wanted to know how she could make such a stereotypical, judgmental statement without ever being there. My good friends tell me, she replied with brio, as if her friends were oracles on top of some alp. With the afternoon waning, we finished our beer and left, tipsy, stumbling back to the Mandarin Oriental, the extravagant hotel paid for by Jack's parents as a wedding gift. Sunke didn't say goodbye in English or German since that would be superficial. Later, I told Jack: she gets her theories from television and films; it's the same place we get our stereotypes about Germans.

Was Connie being superficial with me, being nice because she wanted me in her club . . . only here because I had twins? Of course. Or did she really want to get to know me? Probably not. I knew nothing about her except her children's stats and that she bubbled with good cheer and there really isn't anything wrong with that. I guess I'm more of a realist. If I feel bad I let the world know it. Jack just thinks I'm antisocial. I tell him I'm sometimes a difficult person to be around and he fell in love with me despite this personality flaw, and he doesn't try to change me either, which makes me want to change all by myself, do it on my own, show Jack that he does make me a better person, he completes me . . . blah blah blah retch retch retch. I don't feel comfortable around new people and Connie "Cheer" proves Jack right.

In the end, a nurse bristled in and said good afternoon to Connie as if they were best friends who needed to do a lot of catching up on what the other had been doing with herself for the last month or so. Connie stood up, came closer and handed me a small baby-boy-blue card with her name below the club's name, *President* in italics preceding her name. Please call me, she said, when you get out of here and things settle down a bit, as if they ever do in the baby business. She said goodbye to the nurse by name, Katherine, and left the room with her rain slicker rustling like a sheaf of falling paper.

* * *

After a while the stress of hospital life grew to a near-distant memory and I was caught up with the juggling of responsibility. The two boys kept my heart racing and my body twisting with ache as my surgical incisions healed and the scar grew less angry. Jack and I wanted to share equal duty with Axel Gregory Turner and Perry Joseph Turner—Axel and Perry being our grandfathers' names. Axel was born with a quarter-moon-shaped birthmark below his right ear and Jack kidded around that the mark would make it easier to tell them apart. I kept repeating to him, equally droll, in my own way of joking in return, that they were fraternal and wouldn't look anything alike after a couple weeks. Even then, Perry was so much smaller than Axel.

The first two months they always needed something. Perry would cry and Axel would imitate and cry louder, already competing against each other for our affections, and something I wanted to squash from the get-go. My breasts remained swollen and raw; feeding both of them sapped the milk out, bottle after bottle. I felt like a camel in a desert whose hump was being weaned of water, the sustenance of life, without a replenishing oasis in sight.

In another two months I'd go back to our business part time. After working in advertising and a larger design firm, Jack and I left to open our own kitchen design company four years ago and the workload remained steady if not altogether fully loaded, and didn't drop too precipitously during the outset of the current recession. We scrimped like everyone else we know and started to save even more when we first learned I was pregnant. Bought in bulk, ate in, one great weekly stew or soup—during the pregnancy I craved mild Italian sausage, vegetable and cheese ravioli soup—to last most of the winter weeks my belly grew larger, cut entertainment down to Instant Netflix, caught up on all the British great book adaptations of the past forty years, watched every possible version of *Jane Eyre* available. People liked to renovate, change their plans, stay home too, when times were bad, because selling and buying a new house was such a risk in uncertain times like these. We looked at all jobs no matter the size, remodels, big or small, from RV Airstream tweaks to grand social-climbing McMansions dotting the former Michigan farmland pastures. We had great marketing, something Jack excelled at in his former Detroit advertising agency, and it helped that Jack spoke computer and could design his own websites as a side business. We got the word out in a constant off or online stream, sold the garment, as one celebrity liked to say—we're both fixtures in the downtown blocks, knew the neighboring merchants by name, cried when we watched another storefront become vacant. But right now this was turning around. Two new restaurants down the block, a print shop with hand-made invitations, another law office. Wish us all luck.

It was a beautiful spot we chose to set up shop: the second story over the town's busiest community-gathering deli, where the owners, a couple who apprenticed at Zingerman's in Ann Arbor, served the best East Coast-style Reubens. Two people can only work so fast, and now, with the babies, Jack had to keep the store running alone until I could get back on my feet. He wouldn't let me work at home and I wouldn't let him, either. Sometimes I had to remind him of that little thing called *equality*.

One afternoon, when I was in the middle of changing Axel's diaper, with Perry grinning, dribbling, waiting his turn, the phone rang and I was so glad I let the machine answer it. I could hear the processed voice of Connie Yonker spill forth into the nursery from the master bedroom's answering machine down the short hallway: "Hello, hello. Mrs. Turner, this is Connie from the Mothers of Twins Club and I wanted to catch up with you about our group's next outing. I enjoyed talking to you a while back and wondered how you are feeling now that the worst is over. Give me a call. Best to the boys. Bye, bye."

I didn't remember giving Connie my telephone number and I wondered if her network of informants included all of the cell networks, Michigan Bell and the surrounding state and government agencies. Like a fact checker for a newspaper, she probably had my family background screened so that no surprises would pop up if I became inducted into her twins club during the cloak and dagger ceremony in the basement of the borrowed Elk's lodge. Would she find out I was sent to the principal's office in the seventh grade for throwing a Twinkie across the music room during chorus practice? She couldn't possibly want someone with such a tarnished reputation for reveling in slapstick comedy. I'm the lady who jumped into mud puddles to see if she could splash Jack's pants. Of course I ran after I did the deed, and I knew if I got caught Jack would do something later to get back at me like throw a pie in my face; we'd impersonate Lucille Ball and Ricky or the Three Stooges at the drop of hat or a bonk to the head.

I put Axel and Perry to sleep, planning to feed them as soon as they cried out. Getting two children to sleep at the same time was always a little tricky, most often impossible, but I guess I couldn't complain because I didn't have anything else to compare the experience to. They were my life now. Nothing could stand between me and Axel and Perry and Jack. I looked into their crib and pictured the changes to come, as if I could instantly will them to adulthood with a touch of my hand. We'd converse about their childhood spent in the struggling, economically devastated state of Michigan, working jobs in Ypsilanti, Ann Arbor, Detroit, a few over the bridge to Windsor, Canada, Birmingham, and as far away as Traverse City, Harbor Springs, Petoskey, Charlevoix, up in the northern waterfront homes once word of how good we were, how reasonably underpriced we were, started reaping more and more referrals, anything to pay the bills and keep the family machine well-oiled—their childhood would pass so quickly. All the hours I thought about them when they were away at school or sleeping in their tiny room with cartoon characters painted on the ceiling—their two cribs would soon turn to bunk beds, and until they (I'm wishin' and hopin' here) departed for college themselves, they'd share a room in our cozy two-bedroom cottage in the at-one-time rural woods of Rochester Hills.

Of course not, I'd tell them, I have no regrets, let them know they were my entire world. I'd tell them the mundane facts, that we had to buy two of everything and start watching our expenses even more when we brought them home for the first time, try to teach them to be thrifty like our parents—all four born in the thirties, children of the first Great Depression—had instilled in our makeup. My father told me too many times how he knew how to stretch a nickel until it wept.

Can you tell that I was anxious to get back to work? I knew a lot of new mothers felt like never returning to work after giving birth, and many don't, but I wouldn't survive the home life. All the housework and cooking and shopping would take longer because there'd be more time to do them, and then Jack wouldn't feel so inclined to shoulder half of the burden. I'd get hooked on a couple soap operas and daytime talk shows and never lose my twenty pounds because I liked to eat when I watched television, which is the reason I only watched the becoming-ever-so-obsolete evening news, or the planned family Netflix movie—and, now, there's not enough time anymore to catch up on my period dramas. I had become a sucker for scripted sitcoms too, the well-written ones that have no laugh track and blame Jack for this since he always had great taste in comedy.

The phone rang again and I ran to the master bedroom to pick it up quick because I was close to it and I didn't want the ringing to wake the boys.

"Hello?" I whispered.

"Well, hello, hello. I didn't think I'd catch you. You were out just a minute ago when I left a message for you."

I didn't say anything, but I was thinking: why are you calling me two times a day?

"Did you get my message? I do hate talking into machines, but I only do when I have something important to say." She paused and I still couldn't catch my breath. I found myself inhaling and exhaling deeply again for the second time while speaking with her. The pause wasn't long enough for me to start talking anyway and I did think she'd make a great telephone solicitor; her self-absorbed pacing was perfect.

"A group of us girls from The Club are planning a trip to the local cable station for a tour and a chat with the director of programming. I think it's a good chance to air our views on how violence on television is ruining our children, staining their childhoods, and we both know we have a lot of children to protect. Would you be interested in joining us next Friday? It wouldn't take long; there's just a small tea at Tamara Dashwell's house afterwards to talk about our main topic."

She didn't have to add the word *twins* to let me know that's what would be talked about and my mind was reeling from the effusion of goodwill coming through the phone line.

"I don't know what I'm doing next Friday." I felt my mouth

go as dry as fall leaves. My tongue stuck to the roof of my mouth and made me feel like I had just taken a bite out of a peanut butter sandwich. Why would I even say such a thing? I quickly added, "I have to take care of the boys."

"Oh bring them please. That's what I was calling back to tell you. No problem with that. We allow mothers to take their twins to every meeting until they're in school when it won't be a problem anyway. There's one other new mother coming and it would be a perfect time for you to meet people in the same situation as you. I don't want to be pushy, but I do think you'll find the meeting informative and fun. That's what I stress: fun."

I guess I said okay to bring the conversation to an end. I couldn't very well say no after her wonderfully manipulative speech, and who knows, maybe I'd learn something.

"Great. I can even send one of the girls to pick you and your boys up. Carpooling is the right thing to do with the environment going haywire and all. Next Friday morning at ten. I can't wait to see you again. Bye, bye."

After that I couldn't hang up the phone right away. It was like my arm had fossilized during the conversation and I'd need a crowbar to detach the receiver. You'll like it, I thought, it won't be that bad. I'll get to meet new people and Jack will think it's great because it will be the first time I'd be out of the house socially in a long time. What really made me curious was the reason Connie came across as so fake to me. The Sunke Curse raising its red-haired head. Was I really so anti-social that I couldn't see the genuine kindness in her? Had I been working too long at the drawing board to recognize my attitude needed changing? Then again, I still wondered if my house was bugged so that she knew when my hands weren't occupied, and couldn't help laughing at the absurdity. Thinking up devious plots and being paranoid is something a suspense-novel reader loves to do, and I qualify as a voracious book lover. This sprightly woman wanted me in a club I could never leave. As soon as I stepped one foot in her house I'd be brainwashed and sent out as a covert operative. Whenever I learned something new about twins I'd be compelled to report all my findings after being cleared by the sound of a secret, hypnotically placed, password. Perry and Axel would be babies of the mob-run twins club, where they'd have to serve Connie and her girls' every wish. Jack would break the code and come save us all so that there was someone at home to clean the ever-growing stack of dishes in the sink and wash away the crumbs littering the kitchen counters.

* * *

I refused to dress Axel and Perry alike. Jack pushed for matching jumpsuits and sweaters, but I read somewhere that the more you distinguish between your twins the more independent they'll be; each baby boy won't feel like half a person by the time they reach adulthood. I wanted our last name to be the only matching point. Jack grumbled but understood my reasoning. Axel wore blue shorts and a yellow sailboat-imprinted shirt while Perry wore a University of Michigan sweatshirt and red shorts, something I thought would raise Connie's eyebrows since her twins went to

U of M's competitor, just another subliminal jab which wasn't all that subliminal. That Friday morning I wanted them to look special, as if they were the best children in the world. I didn't care how they might act. I wondered if Connie would keep her smile if Axel spewed rice pudding all over her, and knew she'd probably enjoy the experience and tell me how to toilet train them properly while cleaning herself.

When I told Jack about the meeting, he smiled and nodded his head, but wouldn't say anything, which made me even more annoyed. He knew exactly what had been going through my mind all day, the questions about my anti-social standing, getting out of the house, and work; somehow he always knew. You'll be okay, he finally said, and you can show Axel and Perry off. Big deal, I thought. For some reason that corny song from the seventies kept playing in my head: *You don't bring me flowers . . .*

Which wasn't true, but I had plenty of practice acting the martyr, something else I was trying to change for good. No one likes being told to stop being a victim, and Jack helped me all the time recognize this fault so why was I down on him today? Because Jack would never be asked to be in a silly Fathers of Twins Club, and it was as simple as that. If Ned Flanders asked my husband to join, he'd be strong enough to decline.

* * *

At ten o'clock sharp a new green Volvo station wagon appeared. A woman in a peach party dress with a lot of lace at the hem stepped out and introduced herself as Alma Reilly. She told me to please call her by her last name because she just hated Alma. She also told me I wouldn't have to bring my own infant car seats because she'd reinstalled hers the minute she got the word from Connie to come pick me up. I was beginning to think Connie would make a great political advisor, someone elected to help the president with his therapy sessions in front of the nation, broadcast live across the country. Reilly loved the way Axel and Perry looked together and I did agree they were cute. Even though they were both sniffling and needed to grasp a stray cloth diaper to chew toothlessly, they captivated my attention. I had bought a few cloth diapers just to check that process out but that didn't last half a day and I gave praise to environmental issues double in penance. Inside, and for all my pre-baby life, I always thought babies were ugly things, who looked like miniature Eisenhowers or Capotes. Most of them have jowls for days and a rash that won't quit.

Alma, I mean Reilly, drove like wispy cotton candy. Her hands never gripped the wheel, but her long fingers trailed on the beige leather, making turns so smooth I never shifted in my seat. If she wore gloves, this could've been a *Mad Men* filler scene. Maybe she was still drying her painted (a clear gloss) nails. Usually I drove like a Scrambler thrill contraption at a carnival, where all turns mashed you into the side with centrifugal pull.

We talked about Reilly's job as a fashion designer and believe me I was surprised when she told me she was in that business. I thought we could've been long lost twin sisters. Fraternal of course, but anyone in the design line had my first vote of confidence. I asked her where her children were, Matt and Charlie, and she told me they were with their dad at his painting studio. Reilly's husband, Reggie, taught Printmaking at Oakland University, and they were "helping" with a show that needed hanging. I was impressed and told her a little about Jack and the Imagine Kitchens business we started.

Finally, I asked, "What's this club really about?" I then reached behind me to tug Perry's tiny shoes. He squealed a little but loved the attention. Axel watched his brother with shifty eyes, and I tugged his feet too. What I really wanted to ask was how she got hooked into it and what she thought of Connie. When any two people get together they end up talking about someone else behind that someone's back. I always liked to take the roundabout course; asking questions would be a simple way to start.

"Oh, I don't know, I like the women in the group. A few of them I've known for four years now since Matt and Charlie were born. I guess I like the camaraderie and the sameness of the experience. How many mothers of twins have you ever talked to?" Unlike Connie, Reilly actually paused for my responses and acted like a good listener. She didn't lecture either, which was refreshing, because so many others only love to hear the sound of their own voice. Believe me, I've been around that type of person all my life so I can spot them. Reilly was turning out to be cordial and interesting.

"None, although I did have a roommate in college who was an identical twin. Her name was Shelly, and, her sister's name was Kelly. For some unknown reason Kelly lived one floor above because they couldn't get a dorm room together and I didn't want to switch, have to climb one more flight of stairs, and her twin sister's roommate, Robin, from Sweden, didn't speak much English, and wanted to follow the rules laid out for her in her orientation packet; Robin was happy and smiling and we're still in contact in case I ever make it to her country. Have you ever been to Sweden?"

"No. But it's on my bucket list. I loved those tattoo and the girl dragon books."

"Girl dragon. You're funny, Reilly."

"I try. They were so raw. I don't think I could see the films though."

"I hear you . . . the books were enough for my imagination, and good books are another thing we have in common. Anyway, these identical sisters, Shelly and Kelly, dressed alike, spoke alike, took the same pre-med courses, and wanted to live off-campus together the next year. I got along fine with both of them but I thought there was something really strange about it." I had never had a twin and the closeness, the unbreakable bond, was unnerving; I was a bit jealous but not in a way I'd trade places with anyone—jealous of their natural tendency to share.

"Most non-twins do think that'd be strange, the identical thing, but let me tell you I've always wondered what it'd be like to have someone who could be my mirror image. Matt and Charlie are identical and they're doing fine. I think they even speak their own language."

"No offense. I didn't mean to say anything was wrong with identical twins, and you're too pretty to have someone just like you."

I stopped short, thinking I'd really stuck my foot in my mouth, but she smiled and said, "Oh quit it, I'm a pack-horse and eat everything in sight."

"You must have a very high metabolism." I couldn't believe I said that or had gotten this far in a conversation that now didn't sound like me, my normal self. Was I trying too hard now to be liked? Old pattern. Everything I said sounded like a cliché and fake good cheer for fear of stepping on toes, for fear of not fitting in. Already I was changing and I hadn't even met the whole group yet. I envisioned cameras filming our car ride, violins building a little tension into the scene, and the director thinking about how he'd ever improve his artistic standing if all he got to film were sequels to *The Stepford Wives*.

"Did you ever meet Shelly and Kelly's mother?" Reilly turned into a parking garage next to the television station and pointed out that only half the group could make it to the taping, but they'd try to get to Tammy's house for tea.

Finally, she let me answer her question. I was beginning to wonder about Reilly, whether she was hypnotized or just making nice so she could get all the good info out of me to report back to Connie in a small cellar room lit by a flickering light bulb.

"I met their mother only one time, when she picked her daughters up for Christmas break. She had this almost pained expression in her facial features, as if she had a muscle disorder. I thought she was perpetually sad about the dim prospect of Shelly and Kelly ever meeting the right men and giving her loads of grandchildren. They'd have to marry identical twins. I couldn't imagine a lone man would break them up."

"I'm close to believing you're something of a cynic, Ellie." She then told me she'd help by carrying Axel—easier to navigate around the television studio's tight quarters, she said, even though I had a double stroller—I left this in the back seat of her Volvo. We bundled the boys up in blankets, and I slung the diaper-changing bag over my shoulder. Their curious faces peeked up at us and I could tell we all were in for an unforgettable experience.

"I like to think of myself as cautious. In this world, how can I not be? You said something about a taping. What are we going to do in there?" Overcast sky, a wind picking up, and gray clouds reflected along the window surfaces of the seven-story building gave it the look of motion, as if the concrete and steel girders holding the building to the ground were about to take flight. I wanted to point this out to Reilly, but she'd already stepped through the entryway.

When I caught up with her she told me Axel felt wet. We had a little time and decided to change both the boys. We found an isolated bench at the end of the expansive lobby and went to work, quick and clinical.

"Our club is going to be on the Jerry McCormick show." She let this bit of information drift deep and I sought the reason why Connie had neglected to tell me this fact when she called twice. Inside, I applauded her tactical planning. She really wanted me in her club. I didn't know why and couldn't believe it was only because of the children. For all she knew I could be the next mass murderer, baby snatcher, arsonist to hit the headlines.

"I wasn't told that." Reilly's smile, which only showed her two front teeth, pursed into a thin line and her demeanor, the tilt of her head, told me to behave and not cause trouble. "What's so scary about telling me the truth over the telephone?"

"I have no idea why Connie didn't inform you of the specifics. She just wants to help the kids. Jerry McCormick is giving us the chance to speak out on violence in television first hand. He's letting us have a forum. His show is only regional, but it may push the local programmers to do what's right. I mean, we can only hope it does."

I was going to ask her about free choice, play the devil's advocate because I was annoyed, angry at the thoughtlessness, and Axel and Perry were mine, and Jack and I were the only ones who would control their television watching. Connie did mention the children and violence issue but had neglected to tell me we were the guests on a local talk show, one that I had avoided most of my days flipping channels stuck at home. "Why don't we write our congressmen; it would amount to the same thing; nothing's going to change anyway. I don't even like or watch that much television." I don't know why I lied to Reilly. Please, the best television shows kept Jack and I in stitches.

"Your children will."

I loved the orchestration of certain conversations. Reilly was beginning to sound too much like Connie and I wondered if she was second-in-command or vice president or someone with half the power of the leader. Then Reilly said, "Besides, didn't Connie mention we were coming to this cable station?"

I was about to tell her off. They were my children and they're my responsibility, not hers. Who gives her the right to preach to me about what my children watch? All I said was, "Sure she did, but not to be guests on any talk show for the secretaries on lunch break or the housewives at home. No one important is going to be watching us make fools of ourselves. Listen, Reilly, I don't have anything against secretaries or housewives, because right now I'm one too, but you're fooling yourself if you think our message will reach anyone." I wanted to include myself in the cause because I do think it's important to speak up for what you believe in, but for God's sake, go right to the source.

"Okay, but you do make your own choices. And whether or not Connie left out a minor detail, you decided to come because of something. Our club is about sharing experiences and making friends with some very nice women. You can wait here for me to drive you back home. It shouldn't be more than an hour. You can join the rest of us upstairs as part of a group that already accepts you even if you don't quite accept us. Or you can make other choices that take you right out of here by taxi or calling someone else who'll come get you." Her pauses were becoming chronic because I didn't know what to say, and I didn't take Reilly to be the type to make speeches that bordered on teaching lessons; I wasn't one of her kids.

For once in recent memory, I was able to swallow my anger and tell Reilly I'd go with her. I didn't even say it like a spoiled brat. If this really meant so much to her, I'd do it, but it'd be the last time I went out of my way to be fake friends with Connie or her. My stomach flipped back and forth with the tension I always felt whenever I was reprimanded for something. Perry caught onto my feeling and he started to cry in a low tone—I knew I had only moments to diffuse the oncoming wail. We rushed into the elevator, the twins' tiny heads swiveled around and their eyes widened. They watched the doors close and Perry stopped crying when the car rocked upward.

After patting my hand, Reilly told me I'd do fine, as if what had happened in the lobby was forgotten, forgiven, and we were intimate friends again. Maybe I could take a How-to-be-an-uncomplaining-doll course from her on weekends. Believe me when I say I'd never been a social person. This really was like something I'd read about in a self-improvement manual under what not to do when meeting your Mothers of Twins Club for the first time. Since the time I was born people tried to help me do what's right. I swore when I got old enough to know what parenting might be like I'd be a firm disciplinarian but I'd always let the kids tell me their side. I've known too many parents who punish first and listen later or not at all.

When the elevator doors opened on our floor, Connie came rushing down the hall to look at Axel and Perry and tell me how wonderful it was to have me along. She wore a black skirt, a sharp-pink blouse, and her dog-collar waist was cinched in tight by a silver belt, one of those shiny ones that looked like they're made from melted down trophies. Her tan, eager face was somehow brighter with the makeup she wore. Green eye shadow made her eyes shine like planets too close to the sun.

"We're on after Jerry gives some history about our club. Gloria, Theresa, Tamara, Cyndi, Marsha, and her boys, Reilly, Barb, and

Ellie, I'm glad you all could make it." We stood in a small gray room with too few chairs, a security-chained television, and a lot of no smoking signs—Axel and Perry were passed from woman to woman with a lot of coos and "they're such darlings." The other mothers looked at me and smiled as I was introduced to the group. Connie stood on her toes to whisper in my ear that I'd get personal introductions later at the tea. I nodded my head to say I understood, but in my head I thought I looked like a cow being led to the slaughterhouse by the pretty farmer's daughter. She'd tell me to walk and moo this way, and I'd ring my cowbell to let her know I really was trying my best.

One thing I hated was whispering in a room full of people. If I wanted to whisper in front of people, or felt the urge to relate some tidbit behind someone's back, I'd do it in private one on one. It made me feel better, and I hated giving others the idea that I was excluding anyone from our conversation.

A large woman with a headset opened the door to our room and told us to follow her. Then she barked into her mouthpiece, "No, Frank, you get your butt in gear on the second camera and never take it off McCormick's face. And tell Peabody his camera better zoom in tight when the group comes in. Make sure the entire stage can be seen." She waved her fingers to make us line up single file, but Connie stepped beside her. There was only enough room for the two of them in the hallway. Even I had to admit to some feeling of excitement mixed with the anxiety.

The headset woman said to Connie, "We got enough chairs for all of your group since you're carrying the babies, but it's going to be tight up there so don't move so fast you trip on the cables." Connie must've informed Reilly of the space considerations well in advance, and I again gave her so much credit; I felt relieved now at leaving the infant carriers in Reilly's car.

Connie glanced back to see if we'd heard, said, "Watch your step, girls," with a grin, and then turned forward once more. Her skirt had a line of static on the right side and I found myself repeating in my mind the old, early-80s commercial for Static Guard, three disco-dancing women in wrinkled red dresses helped out by the aerosol spray, and I laughed within because no one else but admen probably remembered the jingle. A minute later, as we stood in the wings waiting to make our entrance, a makeup man appeared and applied a light pancake to some of our faces. I was included, and again I thought about how many people helped me do what's right. The man also smoothed Connie's skirt, which made her giggle like a schoolgirl. With a large stage whisper, Connie called out to us, "Break a leg!"

The headset woman held up her fingers. After a slight pause she started counting down from five, withdrawing a finger for each number: five, down goes the thumb bitten to the quick, four, her pinkie with the silver ring flies into her palm, three, her ring finger joins the rest and leaves us with the peace sign, two, her middle finger abandons her pointer, and one, she swings her arm like a flagman to let us through and onto the stage.

The first thing I noticed when I walked out was the lighting, and I wondered if Reilly or Connie noticed the same thing. It was so bright. I could see people in a small row of bleachers through the haze, but the light was almost overwhelming. Reilly'd be cataloguing what the people wore, checking for old styles and the new avant-garde of those who live life with confidence. Instinctively, I put my fingers up to shield Perry's eyes, and motioned Reilly to make sure Axel's face stayed hidden by the blanket. I wondered what a network talk show like Ellen had for lights. I touched my cheek to see if anything had changed, and my fingers rubbed some of the makeup off. When I realized the cameras were pointing right at me, and Perry, my hand came down in a flash and I smiled when the man in the blue suit introduced me.

I was thinking about what a klutz I was. Perry ate the attention up by gurgling loudly. Axel just fell asleep; it must've been the heat, the brightness. Someone from the audience spouted, "Look, Mary, what a cute baby." Was it worth it? Did I really get off on showing strangers my children? Did I have an unknown disease? Axel, in Reilly's arms, woke up and fiddled with his binky, and when Reilly tried to take it from his mouth, he wailed a long cry until she popped it back in. His eyes widened and the pacifier made a circling movement.

We, as the club we were, took our seats on the mini-stage. The man in the blue suit introduced himself to us as Jeremy McCormick, and told us to call him Jerry. His face was too red. If I had to pick him out later in a police lineup I'd look for the receding hairline and the face that could fry eggs. He wore more makeup than a Sunday morning television evangelist.

Connie twittered out a thank you for having us and blushed like a cheerleader whose skirt always flipped up at the wrong time.

I was getting sick to my stomach and I wanted the next sixty minutes to go by like a fastball pitch. I tuned out the lights by staring at my feet and watching Perry fidget in my lap, burp, and immediately fall asleep. The ladies in the audience pointed at us as if we were newly recaptured zoo animals. The spotlight focus made me more self-conscious than I already was and I questioned myself about living in a community like this. Jack and I had always dreamed of moving into a log home far, far away in the Upper Peninsula, away from the traffic of metro Detroit and suburban Ann Arbor, away from drug dealers and death every evening on the news, away from cellular phones and high rent malls, and a baseball team that goes downhill and bankrupt every year. We wanted a place that was safe for our children to grow up in, but it all fell back to finances and who could really afford to throw their careers down the tubes in the prime of their lives?

"Ladies, or mothers," Jerry said into his microphone, one of those wireless foam-topped sticks, "we brought you here to answer some questions about your mothers of twins club." He paused to look at the audience with his mouth open a little. I guess he was trying to look better than he was, someone smarter and wittier, with that affected movement, but all he did was confirm his status as a second-string cable talk show host. "We also brought a surprise guest, Ms. Marti Sellers. She wants to start the round of questions. Would you please stand up, Marti." I glanced at Connie, and I saw her shift in her seat and her face become as red as Jerry's. A dark-haired, pudgy, frowning woman in a noxious floral-print housedress stood up from the front row. I smelled a rat and knew something terrible was about to happen. This woman was the kind of person I'd warn my children about. "Let's start with the President of the club, Mrs. Connie Yanker, from East Point."

Connie interrupted Jerry, and said, "Yonker. With an 'o,' not Yanker." She smiled her dazzling smile to let everyone know she meant no wrong by correcting the host, but her tone was now guarded, her fingers twisted and twirled her rings as if she was reacting to my thoughts.

"Yes. Well, before I turn to Marti, I have a question for you. When did your club start?"

"Right after I had my second set of twins back in the early nineties." She had the profound ability to give the right amount of time to let her information assimilate itself in the minds of the people she spoke to—yes, she had two sets of twins, folks. "I wanted to find a group of people who knew what I had gone through; to share common experiences and talk about the smooth and the rough spots."

"Okay, Marti, please ask your first question." From my vantage point, Jerry, quite a bit taller than everyone else, disappeared in the haze of lights, but I could still see his hand as it stuck the microphone in front of the woman's face. Her frown grew longer and there was delight in her eyes. I thought she'd start to salivate soon.

"Can just anyone get into your club?" I perked up at that question because I wanted to ask it myself.

Connie smoothed a strand of hair near her bangs and replied: "I do all the recruiting myself at the local hospitals, but yes, as long as she's a mother of twins."

The woman told Jerry she only had one more question and said, "What about Penny Crow? She had twins and you wouldn't let her in?" Marti's face formed a point where her lips pursed—her features embodying a needy accusation.

Jerry turned quick-as-a-snakebite to face Connie and I knew he was in on the whole thing. His facial features mimicked Marti Sellers' and they both looked like tomcats on canaries. I had my own guess about who Penny Crow was: someone who didn't come from the middle-to-upper class of Rochester, Bloomfield Hills, or Grosse Pointe.

I glanced down to Perry and over to Axel. They were oblivious yet squirming. Were they picking up the tension on the set? Reilly met my eyes for a second before glancing away. Was she blaming me for being right? Axel squiggled, slipping in her arms, and she paid little if any attention. I wondered if she treated her own children with such abandon. If she didn't hold him tighter, soon, I'd reach over and take him back.

"I don't know to whom you're referring," Connie said in a spiteful tone I'd never heard cross her cheery lips. It was nice to know she could sound different from a pull-the-string doll. "We have a lot of mothers who come and go. I try to keep every mother who's happy in our club interested in staying with us." I followed the eye battle Connie was having with the woman in the audience and I could tell someone, maybe both of them at this point, was not telling the complete truth. Part of what Connie was saying did ring true: she did try to keep mothers interested in her club, but now I wasn't so sure she welcomed everyone with open arms.

It was at this point that Perry and Axel both started bawling. It broke the gloom on the stage and people jittered in their metal chairs. I told Reilly I had to go feed them and whisked Axel out of her hands and headed backstage, stepping gingerly over the cables. I could picture Jack watching on the office's flat-screen television and I grew even more embarrassed. He'd never let me live down this mortifying moment, my escape over the clutching cables, Axel and Perry hooting and squealing unexpected tears of doom, caught on film forever. I knew what I'd miss: a public rip of a woman whose values couldn't measure up to a politically correct group of suburban American housewives, another mean-girl clique continuing after high school ended. One of the cameras followed my progress to where the headset woman waited. I heard her say, "Get that camera back on the President-lady-Yonker's face. This is getting good." I asked her where I could change them; the excitement made us all weary, and their cries lessened once away from the glare of the lights; they remained a bit starry-eyed and nervous. The woman pointed towards the dim gray waiting room.

I settled in a squeaky red leather chair opposite the tiny television with the live show blaring from its tinny speaker. Connie's face stayed on close-up for long stretches of airtime, recording every human frailty, her makeup no longer immaculate, smearing with heat-sweat. She tried to show indignant composure but ended up shouting something about why the club came to the television station to speak about violence in programming, how it hurt the children, and if they didn't stop with the accusations, she'd leave. Jerry asked why she felt so uncomfortable. It was obvious Marti had filled him in on a little indiscretion with the club membership drive. He said, "Is it true your club doesn't allow black mothers of twins, or single or poor mothers of twins onto the monthly membership rolls?" He grinned like a prosecuting attorney, full of sparkling mirth while uncovering political and criminal intrigue.

Connie fluttered her arms and glanced at the rest of the mothers for help. Their heads stayed down, meadow-grazing sheep, and I was very glad to be in the waiting room breast-feeding the boys. Perry finished and was waiting for a burp when I noticed Connie darting out of her seat on the stage and heading off into the background. Jerry cut to a commercial after asking the woman from the audience if she'd like to take Connie's vacated seat. The woman beamed with satisfaction, and I felt like punching her for being so smug. I liked to set people straight, but I wouldn't rub their noses in it like an egotistical contrarian.

I glanced over when the door opened and admitted Connie. Her features shrunk with gloom when she caught sight of me. The color drained and her eyes no longer looked like radiating planets.

"You must be happy to see this happen too." She waited a bit before continuing. "None of this matters. You don't have to believe me or not. I accept everyone who wants in on my own terms."

"Wait a second, Connie, I never wanted *in* in the first place, on your terms or my terms. You came to me. Remember?"

When she looked at Axel and Perry she cracked a tiny smile even though her eyes began to tear up in the corners, and said, "You have boys."

I tried to understand her words and the sadness in her voice. Was it all an act? She came over to sit down next to me and asked if she could hold one of them. I gave her Perry, but told her he'd be spitting up soon. She said that was fine.

I wanted to speak, but her fragile state made me back down; I didn't want to poke the downed, tranquilized tiger with a stick. She peek-a-booed a bit in Perry's face and played with his tiny, peanut fingers.

"I started the club because I couldn't have boys." There it was. The answer, out loud, pathetic, so ridiculous. "My husband didn't want to try for a son anymore. We already had five girls, and who wanted more mouths to feed be it a girl or a miracle son this time? He makes me feel so guilty for that. I love him despite his constant, inconsolable picking at me, or his close-knit, harping family, but I never will forgive him—spends all his days locked away in his law office, or hunting, or on the golf courses with his wiseacre brothers who tease him all the time because they know he and I are sensitive to it, say that he should've dealt with Anne Boleyn long ago as if my husband was some lost sonless king, the egos in that family astound me; I've witnessed their venom and they can get real sick—my husband says I never know how to take a joke. All my girls are gone now and they barely call home more than twice a month—one, Vicky, she insists on Victoria now that she's an adult, I always have to track down to make sure she's still out there. She's the most resentful, files imagined slights away for future battles, clinically depressed; the others don't like coming home if Victoria's going to be around, haven't had all five of them in the same room in over five years. I sure can have twins, but raising them to appreciate what each parent gives up for them? Victoria, who's also the youngest of my girls, the very same depressed daughter, the most transparent, fake, hates me, hates her father except when he's handing over money, acts like we're to blame for her every unhappy thought. We gave all five daughters a college education—not good enough. They weren't boys, and now that it's captured on video for all time, they'll add this slight to a long list of grievances. Doesn't stop them from asking us for more help, money, support though, oh no—they'll lay on the guilt as thick as Michigan humidity." I didn't want to hear anymore. All I wanted was to get out of there, and go wait for Reilly in the lobby. She'd crossed into a place of unraveling I couldn't follow—and she'd been trapped in this place long before today.

I asked her to hand Perry back so I could wrap a blanket around him, and then said, "Couldn't you have gone for help instead of creating this fantasy? Hire a family counselor?" I didn't know how she and her husband lived day by day, but after decades of reading advice columns, it felt like a logical thing to say to her. It would take a long time for any counselor to tackle all the issues she'd just listed.

"You won't be coming back, will you?"

I didn't think I needed to answer, and she didn't want one. I said, "Can I ask something else?" She regained some control, pulled tissue after tissue out of her purse. The credits were about to roll on the television screen so we didn't have much time before the other mothers of twins joined us. "Do all the mothers in the club have boys? Is that the membership fee, so to speak?"

Connie nodded her head, said, "Not officially, and not at first, and I'm not against girls . . . Candy's still a member. Her identical girls, Rhonda and Felicity, are both at Penn State." But she stopped there with no recent mothers of twin girls she could mention.

I wanted to ask her what she did to mothers of split twins, of girl and boy, but couldn't. Even in a club for the mothers of twins it was a man's world. Reilly came in and curtly asked me if I was ready to leave. She told Connie, without looking at her at all, she wouldn't be going to Tamara Dashwell's tea, gathered Axel into her arms with my approval, and shut the door behind her on the way out. I stood with Perry, and squeezed Connie's right hand. All the way home, in Reilly's silent car, I wondered how long Connie sat in the waiting room, staring into space, thinking about her five resentful girls, about boys . . . twin boys, identical, fraternal, compelled to gather with their mothers, running rampant over rolling Michigan hills with feral glee.

When the Ship Sinks

Everyone on board wanted the ship to sink. Of course, I only mean that, with all the unmotivated inertia walking into every cabin or suite (personal butler included)—the relaxed frowns on so many pusses that said: "Keep your distance, punk!"—I just came to the conclusion that everyone wanted *Clarion Of The Seas* to go right to the bottom. Remember playing dot-to-dot? That's my every waking thought now that I'm single. I was so aware of this cruise-ship ennui because I was at a low point in my own life: almost forty, and newly divorced because my ex-wife, Chandra, said I didn't pay any attention to her. She knew better than to say I wasn't still in love with her.

We couldn't have children. I'll take the blame for this since, after a lot of money spent and an emasculating examination, I, everyone—my wife of course did the telling to the wives of my coworkers, dropped that little private bomb so much some of them started with practical jokes, anonymous of course—found out my little men were weak swimmers. For the last three years of our six-year marriage, and right up to the time she moved out, Chandra had that clock ticking so loudly its alarm woke me up most nights.

I worked a high-pressure marketing job for a firm in Atlanta, the fastest growing city East of the Mississippi, where all the people my boss hired came straight out of top schools, and had brilliant ideas, a fresh outlook on consumer orientation; and, as time passed, increasingly, was something I was afraid I lacked. The other partners wouldn't say anything directly to me, but I heard through the office grapevine that I was burning out; then again, I also heard I had somehow contracted a terminal illness post divorce. Am I wise to listen to gossip? I only grew puzzled over who planted the lies. Here I am running away again, taking my accrued vacation time, using the cheap, singles cruise I bought and paid for before the bottom dropped out of my portfolio.

Bottoms up, cheers and all that. I told, and tipped well for it, one of the many darting, eager-to-please waiters from the Philippines, to keep my margarita glass fresh, filled and salted.

There were a lot of people on board who leaned over the railings and stared for hours at the churning blue water below, next stop some island named after a Saint. These people didn't even stir when the social director called for a shuffleboard contest with updated for-randy-singles-only rules—which sounded more like strip shuffleboard. Even the afternoon exercisers on the jogging track seemed sluggish. They looked like mind-controlled zombies. Someone actually closed his eyes and started to fall from the quarterdeck, but was saved by a woman who was, apparently, his wife, even though this cruise was billed as for the unattached only. The man yelled at the woman and turned away. His Hawaiian-print shirt ripped down the sleeve and the woman held in one hand the tattered remains. The woman shouted, "Don't leave me, Darrin." I hear you, lady; been there, done that, and here we are.

I strolled up to the Water deck where the outdoor pool was and spied an empty lounge chair next to a large woman wearing polyester pants and a matching sleeveless, diaphanous peach shirt who also had a towel covering her face. I sat down on the chair. The plastic beveled in the middle. The rather tall prone woman lifted a corner of her towel to see who was invading her air space. I looked her in the eyes, and they were pretty, a light green; she pursed her lips and let the towel drop again, probably sizing me up, equally categorizing my physical flaws. I wanted to offer her some sun block.

Some people discriminate against the overweight, but I don't. I call them like I see them; there are nice fat people and there are mean fat people, and I don't think I'd be best friends with anyone who was mean to me for no reason. Heck, even I could stand to lose a few pounds around the middle, but I know I can't help my genes or my food intake, the two things that make me look the way I do. That was another thing Chandra couldn't understand; she even brought it up in court to try to embarrass me: "He eats too many *business* lunches, comes home, won't eat what I fix him, and won't exercise anymore either." The judge didn't accept her plea of divorce because of cruel and unusual punishment, but he let her have her way because she said I'd abandoned her. She got the good car, my red 1973 Porsche Carrera, the cabin on Lost Lake, and the resentment-built longing for imaginary children the rest of her days. The lady next to me should be happy I took an interest in her at all.

The sun beat brilliant heat onto the deck and I glanced into the swimming pool and was blinded. No one swam and no one even appeared to be interested. The water was probably at the boiling point.

I needed rest and relaxation. This singles cruise had been my boss's idea. He said the pressure was getting to me, that he needed his senior partner to be on his toes for the marketing deal with Popular Phosphorescence, a new competitor to GE in the Southern states. Take one of those cruises, we get the employee discount, he said, and then gave me a brochure with the 1-800 number circled. I've been on several, he said, and I wanted to know if he'd taken his wife with him, another woman with major issues ever-willing to pick a fight with anyone not quick enough to pay attention to her needs. She liked me though, always stared me right in the eye at the Christmas party, told me she could tell I was one of the few honest men left in Atlanta—would always ask what my wife was up to . . . simple flirting I always resisted, and I played the Jerry Lewis buffoon in her clutching presence, "let me get you another glass of champagne" . . . she made me nervous, her avaricious nature, I found myself searching nervously over her shoulder for her husband to suddenly appear, come over and see her making a play for me and her switching it around on me just to cause drama.

So there I was, relaxing. I had just finished the morning tour of the ship: starting at the Bridge, where the captain eagle-eyed us into keeping our hands in our pockets, the Signal Deck, Sports Deck, Boat Deck, where the lifeboats seemed dusty and unused, unchecked for months, then down into the kennels, where small, yapping, accessory dogs the owners couldn't part with were kept; the Theatre Bar, where we stopped for a morning Bloody Mary; the Casino, empty and still confetti-strewn from the night before with one college dropout sweeping up garbage in the far corner;

a short walk to the tiny Library, the Bank, the Nightclub, again empty and being tidied up by another college clone, and the ever-present Philippine Busby-Berkeley crew, the shopping Arcade, the Florist Shop, where a woman in her sixties was haggling with the lady behind the register about the price of genuine Moroccan baskets, another bar, more drinks, and then breakfast at the Buffet Bar outside near the miniature golf course.

I sat with a woman who smiled a lot and told me she was from New Jersey, but worked in Manhattan. She wanted to impress me with her credentials right away, get things off to an even, equal setting in case I tried anything else besides admiration. I told her there was no such thing as safe sex anymore and that I was impotent and took the cruise to recover from a failed prostate operation. "How awful," she said, and industriously went back to the pastry table. She kept her face in her plate until the guide called for us.

During the next part of the tour, the lady stayed well in front, smiling at the cheesy tour guide, one of those chipper Ryan Seacrest types who always had something witty and rehearsed to say about the current addition of the Gymnasium, all the latest step climbers, and the indoor spa services. We wound our way through the bowels of the ship, covering the crews' quarters, Launderette, boat lift, Barbershop & Beauty salon, Engine room for a quick peek at all the hard work that keeps the ship happy and the guests in motion, the Hospital, Wine Cellar, and the Chapel, where I wanted to scream for the fun of it.

The last place the man led us to: the viewing deck above the anchor, which was larger than a Ford station wagon, painted white, and nestled into the side. The final thing the tour guide gave us: an informational bit of doom talk. He let us know about the plusses the ship had in case of emergency. He said, "The main bulkheads are the steel walls running athwart ships on the *Clarion Of The Seas*, and they are normally watertight. A collision bulkhead is a watertight bulkhead near the bow to prevent flooding in the event of a collision." He pointed to the right like a game show host and continued, "The metal shields on the berthing hawsers are to prevent rats from coming aboard, and those shields are called rat catchers." He seemed to be sparkling from the information he was giving us, making us think about ships colliding with icebergs or other ships or nuclear submarines, making us think about rodents scratching through the cabin walls and chomping our shoes. He didn't have to tell me the ship was full of rats; I already knew it.

Besides, who was this guy anyway, I'm sure he doesn't know what athwart ships or hawsers mean either. He's the type you run into every day who tries to use words larger than everyday life. It's a power thing. I do it in my job to impress clients. Sometimes it works and other times the client knows even bigger words, and corrects your misusage.

So I relaxed, took a few deep breaths. Now that I'd taken the tour with a lot of other single people with nothing better to do, I wanted to sit in the sun all day and bake, make myself invisible and watch out for someone who looked like I did: divorced, vulnerable, cynical, confused about where life was going, and stuck in a job as exciting as building Playdough houses.

A little while later I saw a thin old woman in a mauve bikini made only for sculpted models hobble over to the pool. Her skin, deeply tanned, looked like fine alligator hide. The glare from the water didn't bother her as she sat down on the edge and dipped her stringy legs slowly into the water. She just stared at the sun-dappled water like all the others. Her arms stayed snug against her body and her hands rested flat on the pool's edge.

A cocktail waitress passed by and I waved her over so that I could order a drink and perhaps learn her name. My personal waiter had vanished for some irritating reason. My travel agent, I mean, the automated cheery animation from the travel website, had told me that the worker to passenger ratio was around four to one and that everyone was out to make my cruise very special. I wanted the cocktail waitress to make my cruise unforgettable but she took my order for a pineapple margarita like a robot, turned around and left without telling me her name. The short shorts she was wearing undulated away from me and I sighed heavily. The giant lady who was probably on leave from the circus lifted her towel again and pursed her lips as if unaware she was even making such a dour expression, as if this was her natural state in the wild. I'd fire my travel agent if such a thing as a travel agent still existed.

The old lizard woman by the pool took off her sunglasses and flung them into the water. I saw them dip and twirl on top for a few seconds before plunging to the bottom. The glasses were made of plastic and I wondered why they sank before I realized they must be prescription sunglasses. The woman must have very bad eyes, or a nictitating membrane like any other reptile, but she just stared at the pool water as before, brilliant turquoise, not squinting at all.

The towel lifted and dropped again beside me. I heard an audible grunt as the woman tried to roll over onto her stomach. The plastic of her lounge chair screeched with tension. I turned the other way so I wouldn't have to watch.

The old woman by the pool hunched her shoulders forward. The cocktail waitress returned with my drink and I forgot to ask her name as I gave her a generous tip, which wasn't even necessary on a cruise until the big bill came due, but, somehow, I always carried singles and felt better doing so even if it made me look like a newbie dork cruise passenger. Her shorts rode up her thigh as she bent over to collect three empty strawberry daiquiri glasses next to my lounge partner.

A gull with black-tipped wings flew by overhead. I wished I had that kind of freedom: to fly over a great expanse of water, stop for a rest on the lookout tower of a huge water-plowing vessel, search for a really exciting destination, something new, be able to change directions at any time, and then take off again, wings folding, pumping the speed into something more than longing.

The book I had bought in the gift shop during the tour was yellow with age. It was a mystery novel about an old man who traveled from one country to another trying to find an answer to a children's riddle painted in red, blood, on wallpaper at the scene of his best friend's murder. I figured out the riddle after twenty pages and, in disgust at the simplicity, lobbed the book at a baby-blue trashcan five feet away. In the sun, the flap of the book cover and pages made it look like one of the gulls until it bounced off the side of the trashcan and landed with a 'ka-thump' on the deck.

A deeply tanned, hairless little person ambled by the trashcan. His two black marble eyes watched everything, shifty and hard. When he caught me staring at him he took a deep breath and puffed his small but muscular chest out like a strutting baby rooster. He walked over to the mystery novel and picked it up. Bored, I told him, "The mortician did it." The words just came up from that steel pit inside myself, the one I tried to keep hidden away, and the one that formed after my divorce was final, when relationships became ideas in a theory class.

The small man, and the towel-peeking woman both grunted resentment, the way Atlanta strangers display coldness to anyone who interferes with the status quo. With a sigh, the man came back to the trashcan and let the book tumble in. He wandered away, his face even more intimidating, posturing, strutted over to the other side of the swimming area near the windscreen.

The old woman slipped into the pool, leaving a ripple as her pecan-shaped head disappeared below the surface. In retrospect, it was a beautiful event. The woman sliced the water and left nothing behind but a sliver of water, filling the surface with a remnant of motion, quiet, dignified, and wondrous; the same feeling came over me, the one I get while watching sleek dolphins or killer whales jump and pierce the froth, magnificence in nature, a purpose and clarity in design. The old woman seemed to relish the feeling, the control of the water; her arms were the last to flow beneath the surface. They were entwined, her hands open, fingers reaching to the sky.

Another black-winged gull flapped overhead and dove into the sea. My mind flipped back and I imagined myself as the gull taking the plunge into the cold blue spray, in search of the click of light that attracted it. What it must feel as it struck and rose, brushing its wings back and lifting to even greater heights above the ocean, above the ship, only thinking of survival. How it must be like to live only by compulsion.

The man in the Hawaiian-print shirt strolled onto the Water Deck, glanced furtively left and right, raised a leg over the ship's railing and followed the gull into the churning water, bobbing and twirling in the wash. I watched him and thought he was thinking the same thoughts, had the same drive to find out what it's like to fly to new heights, unburden himself of life's constant checks and balances. The woman, the same one who had ripped his shirt before, came running up the deck stairs shrieking the words, "Overboard! Man overboard!"

A loud siren sounded and stopped. There was a large whoosh of air and motion as the ship started to slow. Yards, football fields of length passed, miles of distance, from where the man had jumped. The ship's crew rushed here and there—clowns, I say— bumped into one another, and leaned over the railings. I wondered if the ship would tilt and start to sink if everyone rushed over to the port side to watch the rescue, all at once, all that weight. It was like that idea they told me about in school when I was a kid, about what would happen to the world if all the people in China jumped into the air at the same time and landed, all at once. When the ship sinks I'd be damned if I'd wait for all the women, especially the one next to me, and children first, even though there weren't any children on board, before scrambling into the nearest lifeboat.

The cocktail waitress scampered past my lounge chair, heading for her emergency station. As she passed the pool, she let out a shrill screech. The pecan-headed woman had her prescription sunglasses back on and her body floated limply in the chlorinated water. No one dove in to get the body. It was the ship's responsibility, and the ship's crew was busy trying to find out what to do about the overboard man. I don't think anything like this had happened on the cruise ship before and I pictured the captain flailing through the ship manual: Is this situation under E for emergency or P for panic? Other lounge lizards circled the pool, stared at the body bobbing along the blinding surface until my lost waiter made a sudden reappearance and leapt into the pool to retrieve the old woman's body, drag it to the deck with help from the crowd, and start CPR.

The oily-suave rooster man strutted over to the cocktail waitress and put a comforting arm around her. The cocktail waitress slapped him on the face. She rushed towards me, screamed, "You saw where *he* touched me!"

More sunbathers gathered around the pool's edge. All of the heavy pressing, the occasional mouth-to-mouth: "Stay back, stay back! Give the man some room . . ." And the drowned woman sputtered back to a new life with her frantic, throat-constricted word: "Sunglasses!" She, along with her rescuer, will dine at the Captain's table tonight, crack crab shells and eat lobster manicotti and laugh about how short lifespans are. Another gull flew by and landed on the white lip of the pool. The bird's head moved from left to right.

As the cocktail waitress stood in front of me, her hands posed on her hips, I said, "I saw."

She then waved her arms, made geometric patterns in the air, and said, "Can you believe all this shit?"

I just inquired what her name was.

She didn't tell me. I was relieved I hadn't offended her. The little man ducked behind the pool, and the gathered crowd, like a magician's rabbit.

The giant (and now supremely peeved lady who certainly was lacking that little thing called empathy—I almost told her to try walking in someone else's flip flops) with the pretty green eyes who had a penchant for strawberry daiquiris, and who wrapped herself up like a summer mummy in diaphanous peach, grunted in her lounger next to me as if her first impression of me was once again proven right.

She said to the waitress, "Since you're just standing there with nothing to do, I'll have another drink, and you can tell whoever runs this tin-can outfit that they better be handing out discounts by the time we get back on shore." The waitress opened her mouth but closed it quick, smart girl, and walked back to the pool bar. I didn't ask my lounge partner how emotionally scarred she felt, but we sat there for hours and watched the show despite ourselves.

Poseidon Eyes

The water is a part of me, a passion splintering my vision; it has always been a part of me. My name is Melanie Fortaine, and I live a life hidden by crashing waves along the California coast; it is where the dueling began. Everyone around me has changed so much and so often I appear to be unyielding and resolved; it's the choice I made. I'm a college senior now with one more summer season to drift by before I go back to my marine biology books, lecture paper, and honors thesis recording the influence of kelp beds on shark migration in the San Francisco Bay.

Last week I turned twenty-one and my parents set up the usual week-long stay at the Break Wave Hotel to celebrate—my mother always says she loves my summer birthday and I deserve a lavish celebration. I know that's only partly the reason. The other part being her constant need to be seen as a kind of queen amongst her wealthy circle of friends, the party becoming more intricate with diverse themes and an increasing budget. In the current economy I told her a slice of my hometown pizza joint's to-die-for leek and potato pie would suffice, just the three of us, but mother wouldn't hear of it. I gave in once more, but even so, I told them I'd be a day late, what with the drive down from Berkeley, where I was interning for a marine biology, green initiative, environment-driven corporation specializing in extracting toxins from any polluted body of water, and, yes, these companies do exist; we're not all in thrall to harsher corporate mind control. My mother sent their longtime driver to pick me up; they wanted to make sure I could still be trusted, to keep a watch on me; they thought I still had delusions even after all this time, water under the bridge. I haven't let it slip, not even once, that my delusions never went away. When your world changes you learn to adapt.

I make Jeremy stop at a branch of my bank. I have a check to cash, a present from my Aunt Evelyn. To me, when I enter the cold marbleized interior of the bank, all the tellers look the same: I see them in three-piece suits, ties, dress suits the color of gray, brackish water; their skin is scaly and fishy, cheeks and jawbones encrusted with murky green barnacles. And they all seem to be staring at me with their fish eyes, blink-less, but maybe I'm just being paranoid because everyone always stares at me, as if I'm different, somehow mysterious. It's something I've adapted to; I now get a slight thrill out of it because it boosts my confidence, something I've worked hard to maintain since my low self-esteem became a daily dinner table conversation topic back home seated between Mother and Dad, their bulbous bodies shaking and negating all my distilled energy to bits. I still remember all the different therapists I was dragged to: flippers, gills, sharks, eels, and manta rays.

Since my vision was changed I see money differently. Pearls for large bills, speckled shells, coral for coins I keep in a small opening-eye purse. Whenever I have to cash a check, it takes the form of a clamshell that has to be scrutinized, examined to make sure it's good.

I move to the front teller and hold out a dull, old clamshell. It is large, covered with sea algae and the teller opens it as everyone gathers around. A pearl the size of a jumbo jawbreaker sits on a muscled-red tongue.

"We need two pieces of I.D. for this," says the teller. He grins like a tiger shark, suit stripes flamboyant smooth going down, and razor sharp if you run your hand against the grain.

"I don't have any."

Before I can open my mouth to tell him I always bank here when I'm in town, the man says, "This must not be your regular bank. When you get some, come back to me." I want to reach across the coral-topped counter and point out to him that my Dad could buy this bank a hundred times, but that would be too much like my mother's haughty reaction, and I retreat, remembering humility and money and how it perverts.

The teller pushes the clamshell into my hands and I watch as the pearl falls onto the cerulean area carpet. It rolls out the entrance of the bank and stops in front of my idling car. I can't figure out why the check bounced and then rolled and I begin to draw conclusions, flutters of the past, when strangeness flipped my world, when I had to become fluent in focusing on *his* presence, when I could tell *he* was in the same room with me, watching me, making the hair on my skin stand on end. I have a bad feeling forming in my mind. I realize no one else has noticed except Jeremy who steps out onto the sidewalk, picks up the pearl and hands it back to me.

"When was your birthday?" he asks in a voice mimicking cordiality and caring. I want to ask him to cut the charm out and tell me if he saw anyone weird watching me in the bank, but I know he reports to my parents anything strange I say, anything they can use to buckle me down.

I try to be nonchalant when I tell him, "I thought it was yesterday."

"Well, Happy Birthday to you anyway."

"Thank you, Jeremy. I'd like to go to the hotel now." We are all business now. He holds the door as I climb into the back seat of the green Jaguar XJ6; then he takes the driver's seat. The air from the open windows blows my blonde hair up behind me and I let it obscure the back window. To my left is the ocean. The tide is coming in on the little inlet and small children play chicken with the gently rolling waves. Jeremy watches the water as if mesmerized. Something odd is in the air. Hypnotic. Even though I know this is all illusion, I still leap over the seat to take the wheel because the car is veering closer to oncoming traffic while Jeremy gazes at the churning blue water. He turns to face me, but I'm not shocked or even surprised by his appearance because he has always appeared this way to me. His mouth is stuffed with black seaweed, forcing his jaw to drop, unhinge, and his eyes to bulge. Feeling a shiver of cold even in the hot sun, I sit back in my seat. I no longer care if the man drives safely or not.

Jeremy stops the car in front of the hotel. When he opens my door, I watch the seaweed glisten in the sun as it dribbles down his chin. I pick up my purse and hand him a small yellow-streaked pearl.

Seaweed falls from his mouth as he says, "You shouldn't have. Thank you, I mean. This is too much."

"That's all right, Jeremy. Just keep it. For old time's sake." I feel sorry for him and tell him to get a haircut. I then stroll over to the hotel entrance.

The door opens before I can touch it and I let a pair of walruses, the male horned and the female designer wrinkled, through the door first.

The male walrus tips his golfing hat to me. I wonder what they really look like beneath their masks and cover my mouth when I start to giggle.

I step into the hotel and pretend to be shocked when the lights brighten and a resounding chorus of *Happy Birthday* fills the room. My parents started this ocean-view family tradition back when I had my trouble, when I became so depressed, the mere sight of water, people, made me reach out for any sharp object, when I cut myself to rid me of the illusions. Now I thank God, the only true God, cuts heal over and leave me scars to remind me my life is not made up of interconnecting dreams. I try to put a surprised glint into my eyes, and don't know if I succeed. Some of the longtime hotel workers I recognize wish me well and I smile back at them.

A bearded man in a black tuxedo thrusts a small rectangular box into my hands and fades quickly into the crowd surrounding me. Everything seems to be happening too fast and I want to stop the man who gave me the gift because I realize too late that he looked human. Then I glance back at the crowd and blush. Trying to feel elated, trying to almost cry because they remembered my birthday, I say, "Thank you. Thank you so much." My parents bounce over and hug me as best as they can. My mother never shows me much physical affection so I barely get an air-kiss from the tip of her snout.

"Open it. Open it. Open it," someone begins chanting, making the others join in. The tone rises in volume and the chant soon turns to: "Open. Open. Open," as if all curiosity has lost itself and a commanding presence has taken over, forcing me to try to glance in all directions at once. I close my eyes to block out the leering faces. Then there is silence. Clamor too quickly cut off to be natural. I open my eyes. I remember games I played as a little girl, before I was tutored at home by Mrs. Shotplace, before when Dr. Rutledge grilled normality into my head, before when there were schools of fish children surrounding me on the playground, darting, where everyone moved when I closed my eyes, or when I turned my back to count down from fifty. Red Light Green Light, Mother May I, Hide and Seek.

The crowd has disappeared somehow. Only one person remains.

He is dressed in the same type of tuxedo as the other man, but his face is now shaven and he is a larger, more threatening figure. The man's voice is loud, booming through the empty hotel lobby the words: "Open it now."

I glance at the object in my hand. The box is now a large clamshell, and I'm feeling a dim vibration coming through from within. The lip of the shell forms a taunting ragged smile.

"No." I feel the presence here and try to breathe normally, to not let him see my fear. I'm stronger now and even more determined to succeed. I'm not the same little girl who strolled his beaches.

"But you must. Can't you see, my angelfish, you must."

I bite my lip, drawing blood to dispel the images shooting into my head. With all my might I throw the clamshell at the beaming man. I've aimed for his smug, arrogant smile and . . .

* * *

When I was a young girl of seven, I yanked the plastic arms off my red-cheeked doll and filled them with sand. My mother watched me from a distance and told me I was going to break the doll, and didn't I like it? Dad gave that to you on your birthday, she said, dump out the sand and put the arms back on.

"No, Mom, I want to see how heavy she is when she's full." This was so exciting to me, the concept of weight, why my mother strove to keep hers down even when she was already skinny. I also played around with gravity and threw the doll in the air waiting to compare the "thunk" sound as it hit the ground: weighted and weightless.

My mother sighed. Reopening her novel, she started reading the same page she had just finished. Then she had to reread it again. Scowling, she threw the book down beside her and said, "I can't seem to concentrate today. I'm going back to the house. You come up when you're done playing." I knew she wanted to get back on the telephone with Mrs. Fairfax-Worthington to talk about their next doubles tennis match at the club, who they'd beat and who was opening their homes on the next house tour.

I said, "Okay," and fiddled with the doll's arms, trying to pop them back into place.

"And don't leave your toys down here." My mother turned, slipped into her sandals and stepped away.

"Mom?" I called out to her.

"What?"

"I'm going to collect seashells, but I won't go in the water." She worried about drowning deaths, the mothers she watched on Oprah discussing the loss of their children and how it ruined the family unit and caused more cases of divorce than any other reason. I wonder if my parents would get a divorce if I died, especially now that I'm older and willing to test the matter.

"Okay, Sweetheart." Mother shuffled through the sand. It quickly rose into dune, heavily sloped, leveling off right before the stairs leading up the steeper bluff to the ocean-view house.

I watched her climb the stairs. I thought she looked beautiful up there. With the sun reflected behind her on the cliff side, I thought she looked like an angel, and I wanted to run to her and make her hold my hand and pay attention to me, tell me what it's like to grow up without a parent's touch, tell me she loved me more than anything else, more than new cars, tennis circles, drinking at the club, trips to L.A. and parties at the old, musty "stylish" hotel. "We do so much for you, Melanie. How can you say we don't love you?" And they'd try harder, all the while piling the material goods by my side to make up for lost affection.

The tide was turning. Barefoot, I dropped the doll parts and skipped down to the receding water, my feet digging into wet lip of beach. I wore a peach sundress and wouldn't have gone into the water even if she told me to. The dress matched the one my doll wore.

Even though I was only seven I knew all about the animals living in the sea. Dad had given me a picture book encyclopedia full of sea creatures. I studied the wet impressions curving the sand, searching for movement. When a small dimple of sand started wiggling, curiosity made me thrust my fingers into the hole hoping to find a sand dollar, a crab or an octopus. Instead, I was pulled under. Something had hold of my wrist and yanked me down a dark hole that opened below. Unlike Alice I screamed and got a mouthful of sand.

* * *

When I was pulled under the beach I was too scared to think anything coherently.

My hand was jerked harder. Soon, I fell deeper and landed on the black-and-white marble floor of a large room. Air compression cushioned the fall but it hurt. In the distance, waves crashed against a wall-wide window, blue, green lighting playful and mixing colors and shapes, bubbles and life just beyond. Orange-striped fish swam right up to the glass, puckered their mouths, and gazed at the strange room under the beach. They stared at me. Fish can't blink but I wish they could. It's hard to sleep with your eyes open.

I spit sand out of my mouth and pinched sand out of my underpants. As I ran my hands along my legs, I thought: Mom will kill me when she sees how dirty my dress is.

I walked towards the window and the fish darted off leaving vapor trails of bubbles. In a second they were back, playing a game of petulance and happiness: who could scare whom first. The room was lit with some kind of blue light, softly glowing phosphorescence, but I couldn't tell where the light was coming from. I rubbed my bottom, which was bruised from the fall.

Appearing from nowhere, a man wearing a black tuxedo strolled onto the marble floor, coming closer to me. I backed away, trying to escape like the orange fish. He had a harsh face, with a hooked nose and large black eyes. The man said, "What are you thinking, my precious?"

I continued my retreat until I was pressed up against the glass wall, cold and humid-wet. In the air, on my arms, a warm mist drifted. This is a trick, I thought, a scary one. I'd been told never to talk to strangers, but somehow I felt compelled to speak to him.

"Who are you?"

Rising from the floor, a desk appeared. After he pointed at the ground again, two chairs also clicked into place. The desk and chairs were polished pink, yellow and peach coral.

"Have a seat, pretty lady."

I had heard the word lady before, and couldn't think why this man would want to call me that, but I sat down anyway, gently so as not to hurt my bruises.

"Now–What is your name, my dear?"

"Melanie."

"Do you know who I am, Melanie?"

"No." I wanted to go back, climb the stairs to my house, look like an angel way up high, and sit with my mother, make her hang up the telephone and listen to my story, put my doll back together and rip its head off. I wondered what it would be like to be made of sand. I would be heavier, I thought.

"I come from your history. I live in the water at all time—all at once. I have many names." The man seemed puzzled, his brow lifting, because I was staring away in the direction of the crashing waves. "How are you feeling?"

I fidgeted in my chair, dug my fingernails into the coral armrests. My face betrayed my boredom. I didn't like the man, and was still scared of him even though he talked nicely to me, but I was never interested when my parents asked me basic question after question about how I felt or what I did that day because I knew they really didn't care too much; they'd say, "That's nice, Dear. Would you please watch television or go play with the Green girls." I wasn't interested now that another adult was asking me questions. I thought the water splashing against the window, throwing the fish, was much more exciting so I concentrated on that instead.

"Do you know who I am? Stop picking at my furniture." The man's voice grew louder and the waves roared in response. I stared at the man once more and wouldn't budge again if he could do all that; I kept my jaw firmly shut. I wanted to tear his arm off and fill him with sand, prop him in a corner on my doll shelf.

"Is something wrong, my little starfish?"

I shook my head no. But there was.

"Well–let me begin. I've been keeping an eye on you, my sea rose, for some time now. Ever since you started skipping across my beaches, and I must say you are one of the most exquisite, innocent, delightful mortals I have seen. I want you to stay with me, by my side. You'll grow up under water with every wish fulfilled. And when you're older, you will rule all that you see." He pointed out the window and the scene changed to a land not glimpsed by many: the ocean floor lit up for me to see, but it wasn't one part of it, the vision showed all of it at once, magnified and drawn back with what I wanted to see. It was like sitting on top of a mountain, the highest peak in the world and being able to see the land, the enormity of it, laid out before you like a quilt of green and brown, gray cities and dust. Under the water the colors muted and whisked my breath away. Countless ships, wrecked by storms past decades, littered the floor. All the creatures flew and darted like birds, the water becoming air and the coral the trees they flicked in, between the branches, shadow and light.

I didn't care much for what the man was saying, really I couldn't understand what he was trying to say, but I knew what the word stay meant and I yelled out, "NO." The glass wall became opaque, closet black.

The man plucked a clamshell from an inside tuxedo coat pocket like a magician and offered it to me. I felt my arm moving and the clam placing itself gently on my palm. I watched my body move of its own accord and grew even more amazed and scared by the power I couldn't ever comprehend.

"Keep this then, fair creature of the air, as a token of my affection. One of these days you'll join me of your own free will."

"What? I want to go home."

"You will be mine because I was told you were unobtainable, unfathomable. The creatures of the sea tell me we will dance duels until the end, you and I, but I won't force you to stay because I cannot do so without your consent; even gods have rules they must abide by and games to play, but open my gift carefully. It will change your entire perspective." Then the man laughed without moving his lips, water roaring in a torrent. Only for an instant could I see how he really was, his true physicality, how his tailfin swished the floor behind him and the scales glistening on his forehead. Then I saw black tuxedo approaching and I began to shiver more when I started to levitate.

* * *

Another strange man, someone walking along the waterline at the same time I was trying to dig my way out, was offering me a hand. He helped me out of the sand hole and watched as I ducked my head and raced off in the direction of the private beach's restroom shack. I didn't know what to say to the man who had just helped me; he was someone else I didn't know, someone I couldn't trust. Almost in a state of shock, I kept telling myself I had a nightmare on the beach and everything now was fine. But I held the shell, the gift, in my small hand. I searched for my mother in the sand before remembering she had gone home long ago. The sun was a sliver against the ocean, crimson when it dropped below the horizon and lit the sky, diminishing with every second. The stranger who had pulled me out of the sand hole wiped his forehead and continued his stroll. He was probably watching the beach for signs of more buried children.

When I was inside the restroom, I unbuttoned the front pocket of my dress, put the clamshell in it, thought: I should just throw it away, but then curiosity broke and I quickly took it out. I stared at the lip of the seashell so hard I thought it would open on its own. But it didn't. My fingers pried and scraped at the edges and I kept thinking about how my body wasn't mine, how I still had no control over what I was doing.

I opened the shell slowly, only letting it crack the slightest bit, but that was all that was needed. A bright blue light shot out and pierced my vision, a blurry ache formed in my head. Then the light died. Rubbing my eyes with my fists, I wondered what I'd done. Then I opened the shell all the way and found a pearl split in half lying on the red muscle of the clam. There was a thin strip of paper under the pearl.

The paper was yellowed with age and felt whispery to the touch. At that time, I could only understand the first few words written on the paper: *Now you have Poseidon Eyes.* The strip of paper disintegrated before my strangely tingling vision.

When I returned home to my parents' ocean-side villa, my mother was a bottle-nosed dolphin and my father was a humpbacked whale.

* * *

My mother asked me where I had been all this time. It was almost dark out and she was about to call the police when I walked in covered with sand, the fine granules another layer of skin on my body. I knew that she wouldn't expend energy looking to see if I was safe. The brusque quality in her voice was as close as she got to caring that day.

"How did you get so dirty? What were you doing, Melanie?"

"I was under the sand." I stared at my mother and started to hiccup. "You're a dolphin, Mom. You've changed." I spoke slowly. Her eyes, small and flat, yet sparkling with unnatural glee, opened wide.

She ran her flippers along my scalp checking for bumps. "Did you fall and hit your head? Is that why you're talking nonsense?"

What I saw my mother do to me was a bit different. They were flippers brushing at my hair. It even felt different. My father came into the kitchen. I saw his hands first because they were the same as always: large, tanning-bed even on the palms, and hairy between the knuckles. The head and spine of my father had been expanded, extended, and replaced with the features of a whale. I wondered about my parents, how could two different species mate and make any child, someone like me?

I covered my eyes with my hands, screamed a high-pitched, dreadful scream and ran to my bedroom. My parents stared at each other and my father asked my mother what all that was about.

* * *

I watched the psychiatrist read from his notebook. It was my first visit to this doctor's office and I didn't like it at all. After a few weeks my parents told me I would get better, have fun even, if I went to the doctor, and no, I wouldn't have to worry about needles, shots.

I was still only seven when my parents decided to stop my craziness by hiring the best child therapist on the West coast. I thought about turning eight in another month. Of course, my parents would take me to the hotel to celebrate, as they did every birthday. Further down the shoreline. Next to the ocean. They only sent me to the psychiatrist because all their friends sent their kids. I heard Mrs. Fairfax-Worthington, while drinking with my mother, her Bloody Mary Buddy, say that, "She'll grow out of her problem. She just needs to talk to another adult who won't criticize her. Someone she can tell her innermost secrets to." And then my mother said, "I guess so," and then, "Melanie, stop twiddling around please. Go get the tennis ball I hit over the fence." And the shame of my "problem" was known by anyone my mother came into contact with. In school my friends shied away from me, and I heard whispers about how loony I was. As I grew older, more kids came around me and told me it was no big deal seeing a psychologist; most of their parents did too.

My eyes had dark rings around them, suffocating the deep blue irises I was often complimented for. I closed my eyes because, in the way I saw him, Dr. Rutledge had the pudgy body of an adult male in his mid-forties but the face of a large bulbous yet sleek-nosed electric eel. His long neck snaked out of his sport jacket and sparks jumped onto the floor, sizzling the bargain-priced oriental carpet, something inoffensive to match the cookie-cutter landscapes-of-light paintings hanging from the office walls.

I had found the last month and a half almost unbearable. Somehow my vision had changed and an eel with a sharp row of spiky teeth was calling me young lady just like the man who lived under the sand. I instinctively disliked Dr. Rutledge and found myself clamping my eyes shut so I wouldn't have to look at him.

"Melanie, would you open your eyes for me?"

I did and found the doctor gazing as understandingly as any other electric eel would. I closed my eyes again so tightly shut lines appeared on the sides of my face.

* * *

When I returned home after my session my mother wanted to know what happened. A spray of water burst from her air hole as she talked in her squeak-squeak tongue.

"Nothing," I said.

"Come back here, missy. I'm not paying good money for you to tell me *nothing*. What did the doctor say to you?"

"He told me to open my eyes and stop fooling everybody."

"Well. I think that's good advice."

"But I'm not fooling anybody. He's an eel, Mom. I can show you his picture in my animal encyclopedia. And you're a dolphin. You even eat more sardines, and order extra anchovies on the pizza. I only like cheese." I started to cry. "And Dad is a whale and there's a man under the sand who did this to me and he said he's watching me everywhere I go."

"Stop it, Melanie. I don't want to hear you when you talk crazy like this. You're only going through some phase like those talk shows say all children go through, maybe you're too old for your age. You're just not eating enough or sleeping enough. They say eating more fish helps, the oil does something, your doctor even said so, but you don't like fish. Seaweed also. It's supposed to be good for you."

I stopped crying and stared at my mother's row of tiny teeth. Since I saw my mother as a dolphin, she was always smiling, always had a stupid look-at-me grin on her face. Sometimes I even heard my mother squeal like a dolphin, high and ear-piercing when she found a new piece of sapphire jewelry downtown or when she watched the Tonight Show and woke me up with her shattering laughter. My mother was talking underwater gibberish.

"Can I go to my room now?"

"Okay. But you think about what Dr. Rutledge said. And try to get some sleep. We'll eat dinner later than usual. We're going to Andante's for lobster tails."

* * *

In a year's time, one session a week hadn't helped me. My parents didn't know what to do with me. I started cutting the underside of my wrists, letting the cuts heal and scar before making another incision. I couldn't go through with it though; I didn't have the courage. No one noticed except the maid who washed the dirty red towels, and she was too timid to say anything to my mother. The maid appeared to me as a kind of camouflage fish, blended into the background wallpaper in splendid fashion, and she also wouldn't say anything because she couldn't speak English very well and she didn't have her green card yet. My parents stopped making appointments with Dr. Rutledge.

In school, my teachers thought I was disruptive and destructive. I earned some respect from the rednecks and the other cut-ups, but the rest snubbed me, but always came back to me anyway because they knew my parents had lots of money and they thought my stories about what I saw were funny. My art teacher was especially upset with me when I drew a picture of a lamprey: jawless, its mouth circled with sucking, rasping teeth and wrote the art teacher's name underneath it.

When I turned twelve, my parents decided to hire a tutor to teach me at home. Mrs. Shotplace handed me an English grammar book and taught me how to spot adverbs and map a sentence. In my eyes, Mrs. Shotplace had the face of a puffer fish. She would swallow air, expanding her body enormously, whenever I said something wrong. I decided lying about the things I was seeing was the only way to cope.

Depression overwhelmed me on my thirteenth birthday when my hormones started to change. The creatures around me thought I'd put the worst behind. Everything wasn't the same; I had lived within this undersea world for so long now I was taken for granted, and I was found to be strange and little more than a curiosity; I became withdrawn and had no real confidante to help me through the hard times, like when I was watching a movie and couldn't relate to the two seahorses shooting bullets at the blowfish who wanted to take over the town. Mrs. Shotplace wouldn't be back the next year. My parents were starting me in a new junior high school, very private and selective, and they told me all the time how they had to "grease" a few palms to get "their" schizo kid into the place so I'd better not mess everything up. My mother was now becoming like me for some reason and I think it was the years of emotional trauma my visions had put her and her pride through. She was quieter now and rarely spoke even when spoken to.

A week before school started, I took one last look at my mother the dolphin and my father Mr. Moby and told them I was going down to the beach for a swim. There wasn't a response, only a lifting of the flipper and a short sigh.

The undertow pulled me under and I welcomed it and remembered the sensation of falling; this time I wanted everything to end peacefully as I jerked with the motion like a pulled puppet attached to an invisible string. But then I was coughing up salt water and gazing into the first human face, real nose, eyes, mouth, lips, cheeks, I'd seen in six years. He was a young lifeguard with shiny black hair melding the forehead. He told me I'd have to be more careful when I swam off the beach he protected, smiled at me and even helped me home after I rested for a bit under a red-and-white striped beach umbrella. I never saw him again, the beautiful human lifeguard, but from that moment on my life took a new direction.

My parents noticed the change right away. I was smiling and happy and talking to them constantly now, letting them in on everything I did, but not talking to them like they were fish or mother's friends were incapable of eating anything but mud grubs like the carps they were. Mother took this as a sign of how wonderful the therapist sessions and the private tutoring she planned had really been. She took me on a trip to New York City where the Statue of Liberty became a swordfish caught in the folds of a net, and I wondered how telling that really was. She even let me give her a kiss on the cheek before I went to sleep; one night a year later she even said she loved me and wouldn't think of trading me in for anyone else in the whole world. I wondered how many times before when I had fish-mouth she wanted to do just that. My father blubbered and doted on me as if I was seven again, untwisted, before the change. To him I was still his little girl and he wanted to make me happy. I didn't think they really understood me, but I loved their new personality change as much as my own.

I studied harder in school and even made friends with some girls in my math class. We complained about the story problems and the boys who wanted to start dating us even though they looked like they hadn't even developed yet. My breasts were growing and Mom bought me my first real-size bra. My math friends started inviting me on sleepovers and they didn't even think strange thoughts about me like the kids did in my other school. I saw them as outgoing tropically vibrant fish. My parents relaxed during my fifteenth year and thought they had finally gotten through to me, had put the past to rest.

I graduated from high school when I was seventeen with the top of my class. I was voted most likely to succeed and everyone considered me to be the most independent person in the school.

I wanted to be an oceanographer, to work with the sea and the prizes within. In college I made these plans.

* * *

It's as if I never threw the shell. One second my arm is moving, the clam shell grinning, spinning as it plows through the air towards the man in the tuxedo, and the next second I'm standing in the same position, close to the hotel entrance doors, gazing into the man's coral eyes, thinking about throwing the clam shell at him.

"If you throw that shell at me again, you'll regret it."

"But I did," I say.

* * *

"Do you want to give up now, my little lost manta ray?"

I turn my back on the man and close my eyes. I start to count down from ten.

"I won't be gone when you're done with your numbers. I came to wish you a happy birthday."

I try to keep reign on my emotions, evenly, in control. There is so much I want to say. It's been so long since I was seven, so long since our meeting under the sand that I think of it as a dream, that everything around me is the way it's supposed to be. That I have nothing to fear; he said he played by the rules because there were consequences unmentionable if he didn't. That's what I believe anyway as I open my lips to say, "I can't believe you'd ever come back here." The mantra repeats: evenly, without a hitch, no stutter, I want to be in control. "I used to wonder why you did this to me. I began to believe everyone was like me, saw the same way I did. I tried to forget about you and what you did so long ago. Now I don't even care at all." I ignore the man, keep my back straight as I move, wander over to one of the lavender flower-print hotel chairs and seat myself gently onto the cushion.

"You're very sophisticated now, for your age, my dear." I cover my eyes so I can't see the man hovering in the air above me. I forgot he could levitate and the sensation runs back to me, the feeling of sand gritting down my skin and suffocating, clawing at the beach. "How old are you now? Nineteen? Twenty? It doesn't matter. You're grown now, ready to accept my responsibilities. I'll still want you when you're old and no one wants to take care of you or even see you. I'll still be here for you. If you come with me you'll remain young, immortal forever by my side. It is arranged by the gods—who know how fickle humans can be. The pieces are in check and they're watching me now. Don't disappoint me, my precious manatee, for I hate to lose." The man pauses while a beard grows instantly from his face. "I can look any way you want me to, change to suit your fantasy." The beard disappears and his hair color changes to blond and his cheekbones soften. His fingers roll curls into his new hair.

I can't help watching; it's fascinating, but the hardness in my stomach returns and I balance my gaze on the floor. Suddenly, inside, I am boiling with anger. I want to say, "Well you can't play with me. You can't just treat me like a trophy to put on a shelf to talk about to the rest of your kind," but I didn't because I think he'll leave faster if I don't pay any attention to him. I have adjusted myself to my life and vowed long ago never to have anything to do with the man if he ever reappeared.

"Remember, my sea sprite, the time you turned thirteen? You were so forlorn." His brow is sweating and I can sense the tremble of angst? Or what I would call fear? It's in his manner, predictable. He's pulling out all the stops now. The stakes must be tremendously high in his game. The light in the room dims and a wall lights up in the distance like a movie screen. I can hear the sound of waves crashing. Then a picture forms across the wall and I watch as a younger Melanie, a teenager again, runs along blinding white beach searching for her own mystic entrance to the water. She dances with the edge of the surf, and finally wades in up to her waist. Letting the waves bob her gently back and forth, she coasts along the shore almost out of reach from the undertow. Thinking: come and get me—try to find me, in and out, in and out, bobbing along, belly hovering with surf, rising with the crest, gliding effortlessly, the bubbles dipping and ladling her out farther, passing the line of undertow. Saying: catch me by the ankles and pull me down deep where I won't have to watch anymore, see the world through my Poseidon eyes. She swims out farther with the waves calling her back as they pass in the opposite direction: you must not, you break our rhythm, you will find nothing, pleading with whitecaps, speeding towards the beach to ricochet and journey back with her. The scene changes to show sunrays breaking clouds in the distance.

I glance at the man and understand. He is there, in the movie; about to make his grand entrance.

"Make it stop," I tell the man. He only chuckles and shakes his head no. In my mind, I scold myself for showing him a reaction.

On the film, the younger me, I, slips below the waterline, her arms limply following her body down, flinching. A lifeguard appears out of nowhere, breaking through the waves with precise strokes from his muscular arms.

"That's me, my little sea anemone. You're so pretty and I've come to save you."

Hugging Melanie to his chest, the lifeguard with the shiny black hair sidestrokes to shore where a crowd gathers.

"It's the first time you let me kiss you."

The lifeguard tells the people to move back and then performs mouth-to-mouth resuscitation on Melanie.

"I should've known it was you," I say.

Melanie coughs salt water out through her nose and mouth.

"You were the only one not changed. I saw you as human, while everyone else there had grouper heads or something. Why didn't you tell me then?"

Letting Melanie lean on his shoulder, the lifeguard walks her into the shade of a red-and-white beach umbrella.

"'Be careful,' I said, 'I'm always watching.' Not a big enough clue for you, but enough to play games, and that's what I like to do. Besides, you were still too young, and anyway, I saved your life didn't I? That deserves something." The anger is building within.

The nerve of him. He thinks so little of human life. How can you win against someone like that?

The movie vanishes and the hotel lobby lights come on. A school of rainbow trout waddles up to the check-in desk. I wonder if the man really sees them the way I do. The sea snake behind the counter presses a buzzer and a bellboy with sharkskin appears. He piles luggage onto a cart and motions for the school to follow him onto the far elevator.

My thoughts coalesce. In front of me for the first time in years is the grinning man, god, chess player, whoever, who has tried to create my world; play games with me; control me from a distance. Finally. Take it to the limit and leave. The resolve, my independence, I'd built up within myself over the past eight years since my near drowning has forced a confrontation and I won't buckle in.

"You think you can show up whenever you like. Disrupt my life with your special effects." I stand up and point my finger at the man's face. "Well I'll let you in on something. I didn't know much when I was little, but I've learned to live with myself. I don't care about what you did to me anymore. I have real friends and great parents even if they do look like they live in your watery world. Do you hear me? I couldn't care less if I spend the rest of my life surrounded by fins and gills. I've had plenty of time to get used to it thanks to you, and believe me, I do thank you. If not for your little lifesaving stunt, I never would've learned to appreciate my life and the people in it. If there's anyone else betting against you who's watching us right now, collect your winnings because this game's over and he's lost."

The man's amusement turns to silent fury. I can almost see his true features once again, like a ghost image, the tailfin flies behind him and is controlled once more, disappears. His eyes widen and he grinds his teeth together. For years he has waited until I was old enough to reason with, and now I've become too defiant, a creature of impossible-to-harness petulance. In his gaze I can tell he craves me even more and my heart tightens like it did the first time he called me his pretty lady.

"And another thing, Mr. My Little Fish Shit, I've never been happier than I am right now. I wouldn't even want you to change my vision back. I don't even think you could." I'm running on pure bravado now, and I stop talking so I can catch my breath before giving this away, until I feel my heart stop racing. He wants me because I was made an object in a war by some higher power, nothing more, but I can also feel his longing, and I really wonder if a god so cruel can ever know what the word love means.

"You say these words without thinking. I ask you once more, and I'll keep asking you again and again until your stubborn phase is broken. Come with me."

It is more a demand than a civil question but I answer quickly enough and turn my back on him. Then I say, "Go away."

I take a deep breath and head for the hotel stairs to go look for my parents.

"Excuse me, Miss?" I hear the words and watch the shark-skinned bellboy approach. I think he is kind of handsome; the tough skin gives him a rugged look.

"Yes?" I say.

"A man told me you left this in the lobby where you were sitting. Is it yours?"

In his palm sits a large clamshell. It is white, almost pure, polished to an unnatural perfection.

Cats In Trees

Jacqueline wants to be a tree. Under summer heat, spring rain, or winter cold, she's outside, stretching her arms toward the sky and tilting her face up if she's a redwood that day or dipping her face down if she's a willow struck by lightning. Her favorite color is evergreen.

"That ain't a color," Minnie, Jacqueline's seven-year-old sister, says. "That's a tree. What'd you want to be a stupid tree for?"

"Because they never talk back." Jacqueline is now almost eighteen and smiling at Minnie as she thinks about what it was like being seven. She was an only child then. She had lived in the city. There was one diseased elm bent sideways in front of Father's apartment building. There are more trees in the country, more variety. Then, Jacqueline wishes she'd stayed an only child, a singular tree, alone, standing solid like the rest, forever, and no one could really talk to her; trees never talk back.

Mother remains silent as her daughters speak, every now and then correcting Minnie's grammar. She is a small woman with graying black hair always kept in a long braid. Her mother never cuts her hair. Sometimes the braid runs down the center of her back and at other times it snakes its way around her shoulders, stretching to the ground in front of her feet, where she can fiddle with the end. One of her eyes is distant blue. The other is green, and most people conclude that Mother's eyes betray an inner turmoil. Even Mother's good friends find it difficult to maintain eye contact with her. They remain curious, nervous for a second, and distract the subject by saying, "Look at Minnie. Hasn't she grown," to keep the conversation on safe ground. They never mention Jacqueline. And if Jacqueline wants to be a tree, Mother wants to have only one eye color because she believes she has nothing to conceal. Jacqueline thinks her mother hides in a cocoon where the sheath grows on the inside.

As the three hang clothes on rope strung from one maple to another, two orange and white cats jump to scratch the wet edges of the sheets that almost touch the ground. Tice chases Roadie. Roadie never chases Tice. These two cats grow more frenzied in their play. After bounding into the clothesbasket they mark the laundry with dusty paw prints as they try to climb and finally drag pillowcases onto the grass. Mother chases them away.

Tice and Roadie race up one of the large oaks, and they must be thinking Mother is part of their game; in a crook of the oak, fifteen feet above, both splotchy orange faces stare intently at Mother's swinging braid as she returns to help Minnie re-hang a bed sheet. Tice chases Roadie into the upper branches of the oak, where the leaves hide them.

"Put extra pins on the light shirts, Jacqueline, the wind will drag them off the line if the cats don't get to them first."

"Mother, who was it invented the clothespin?" asks Minnie, as she hangs the last garment.

Mother gazes at the highway stretching into the distance down the hill, hears the leaves rustling in the tree as the cats play, and replies, "I don't know. Probably a man, a religious man . . . and,

Minnie, just say 'who invented' not 'who was it.' You have to be correct when you ask me a question or I won't answer it." Mother grasps the empty clothesbasket and walks towards the kitchen door. She turns, glances at Jacqueline, while their faces fold inward, and says, "Minnie, come in and help with dinner."

"Why do I have to make dinner all the time? Why not Jacqueline?" But Minnie goes into the house, knowing the most Mother will let her do is grease the bread pans, make sure there's enough milk, snap beans, and set the table.

Minnie is happy in her tasks and can't wait for Father to finish eating when she questions him: "How'd you like the dinner I made for you?" and then laughs with pride and an almost tangible sense of being the best daughter a father can have, when Father replies favorably, which is all the time.

Everyone thinks Minnie's an innocent young child, a survivor of hardship, but she knows when to turn her charm on and when charm won't work. Minnie doesn't understand Jacqueline. Minnie also sometimes imagines she's an only child. With a sister who only comes home once a year for Christmas, her imagining is easy to do. Her parents give Minnie the best of everything and never mention Jacqueline when Jacqueline is away.

Jacqueline is home now and has been for two months. Minnie doesn't want to accept why because it isn't Christmas. It's summer and Jacqueline's bags are still unpacked in her small green bedroom. Minnie wants her to leave again and wishes she could give Mother the insurance that ran out, the money she needs but doesn't have anymore to keep Jacqueline away.

At the dinner table Jacqueline begins to revolve her head slowly. She lifts her hands above her ears, screaming as she yanks her hair. Jacqueline feels them climbing her trunk, digging their claws into the meat of her on their way up. Tice chases Roadie. "Someone stop them. Oh. Oh, God. They're ripping the leaves. The leaves. Shredded. Someone help me." Minnie stares at her sister and remains silent when Mother pulls Jacqueline up from her chair. Father continues eating, his vision blurred and drifting over the food on his plate. Mother embraces Jacqueline as she thrashes against her. Minnie's envy grows. Mother purrs, "It's all right. No one can hurt you." Mother leads her away to the bath. "That's it. You're okay. Shush, Jacqueline. We'll wash your face. You have such a nice face." Jacqueline cries, staring at the vanity mirror, watching the cats at play in the tree. Minnie hurls her plate across the dining room and flees the table.

Typecast

I drive my black Pontiac like a psycho; it's what I do well. Kelly, my wife, beside me on the seat, clutches the dash in front of her, twists her patrician face into a knot, and screams her lungs out. I say, "Shut up. I mean it. Shut your face." Kelly buttons her features back into an undisturbed surface. Even I can see she transitioned from panic to calm way too quickly (inside I groan but I don't hear the director yell: Cut!). The audience is supposed to think my fake wife's got more resolve than Joan of Arc. We keep playing the scene.

The camera caught my smoldering, hot-tempered, redneck look as I told Kelly not to look in the trunk while I went to make a final deal in Fowler's Bar, but, no, Kelly wouldn't listen. She had to open the trunk and find my stash and lots of blood over everything (Jessamyn, the chain-smoking and coffee-thin actress—she plays Kelly, daughter of the town bigwigs who married a bad boy—acts the privileged diva on the small, shoe-budget sets, too often, and knowingly pisses off the crew so much with her demands they mutter indignities every time she's called to the set. I guess she used to be bigger in her mind at one time). In the next scene, after a quick makeup check, and after Kelly throws our trust into the air, the little things set me off, I slam the trunk shut and hightail it back home where I'm supposed to teach her a lesson. I am menacing. These fights usually end in gratuitous cable channel sex.

It's easy enough to get into character, to become a backwoods drug pusher and thief with a one-syllable vocabulary. So the slow, lazy writers (on this show anyway—and I once lived with a bunch of life-sucking screenwriters and almost needed rehab afterwards) decide the next progressive step is to turn my character into a rapist, communist, and wife-beater turned mute by her lover's gun; a shot to the throat. Soon the directors will make me a murderer. I have that look. I never said the characters I become have to be politically correct. I can't say I am either.

My long slick black and brown hair is pulled into a tight ponytail; my muddy blue eyes always play focusing tricks, as if I can never stare at any one thing for too long, and a stubble-growth beard underlines my straight nose over razor-thin lips. People in the business say my lips could bend wire, but it's my crazy eyes that hold casting directors back from proffering the gem roles.

My girlfriend, Stace, pronounced like that stuff you spray into a mugger's eyes, tells me to be more—more noticeable. I say that's called mugging and I don't mug for anyone. She says she means be stronger, grow a backbone, you're such a doormat sometimes; she wants me to push my way in, and around (what I call showboating—which goes against everything my acting instructors drilled into me).

"All they give you are these damn hoodlum roles," Stace says as if she once worked for the mafia. "You need to play the lead heavy for once, or an interesting but beaten-down detective on one of those multiplying crime dramas. That's a steady paycheck." I then think, at this moment, repetitively, the door seems to be tightly shut. Stace is only saying this because she's seen the writing on the wall, that the murky series I'm a part of on a second-tier cable channel won't be picked up for a third season. That I'm just treading water.

The television show started two falls ago with a 13-episode first season to test those very same waters. It started with some surprise and garnered a flurry of showbiz accolades for bright innovation in a year of drab rehashes of old sitcoms and drama duds—mucho style and glamour in the back woods of the Upper Peninsula. They filmed from February to June with one-week breaks scattered whenever a new director showed up.

The show opens with still camera shots of cars driving over the Mackinac Bridge, deer carcasses across hunting trucks, then come shots of Range Rovers entering a secluded mansion. The show fills up empty transition time with bears roaming the woods of a stand-in forest; then they shoot straight to a commercial sponsor.

The first time I appeared, the critics called my performance simply one-step removed stereotyping, whatever that means. I get a lot of fan mail from prison convicts, and I was chosen to play Clarence Judkins because of my look. I'm tall, big, but not too big, gut and girth, long, black, stained jeans and lumber boots to kick ass in. My wife on the show, despite her off-screen iciness, is a strikingly pretty red-haired actress from Malibu. She was found, or discovered, years ago now, on the beach during spring break from Pepperdine, by an assistant casting director, and she's got three magazine covers and a truckload of straight-to-video films in the can, but more B-list offers ever since she started getting beat up by me. I make sure everyone knows I donate money to fight

Domestic Violence; that I'm not the character I play on television, but still people shy away from me when they recognize me in the supermarket or pushing a Costco cart. I'm not big enough to pay someone to do my shopping for me.

During the break between the first and second season shooting schedule I got little to nothing, not even a summer film offer to play the mute bodyguard for a former A-lister in a South American action flick (I wanted that role bad). The script called for me to punch Kelly's lights out in the first episode of the second season (make the dwindling audience hate me even more), even if it wasn't for real. Someone has to play these disgraceful parts and I've got the look. Stace says to me all the time the show writers have had it in for me ever since they came back from the last strike. I agree with her; they haven't been doing me any favors and I fear a slow death scene is in the works. I can play dead.

My girlfriend, really my fiancé (but we hardly ever use the fancy term, ever, and that's been a sticking point), Stace, thinks the actress, Jessamyn, and I, had a real thing going on off camera, and I tried to assure her, said to her, how could she even think such a thing. I tell her all about Jessamyn being a prissy diva, but she worries away at little things; it's part of her nature. Stace and I set a date to get married next June after the show wraps for the summer, and she doubts me now. I don't know what to say.

Stace says, "You're a cute teddy bear man. I'm sorry I said that. I know you're not like those people you play on your shows."

"Good," I mumble back, "at least one person in Hollywood thinks so."

I sulk with the best of them and that's why I got to play a brain-dead comatose rapist who wakes up every full moon to cause hell in the small cult film: "Coma Man From Manhattan Beach." It also went straight to video, was played on Halloween night at 2 a.m. on a pay-per-movie cable channel, but I was able to buy a new saxophone and pay the rent for my small duplex in Santa Monica. Stace says we have to get a new, she means larger, place after we get married on the beach with a reception to follow in Laguna. Her father owns a condo in Corona Del Mar, and wants the wedding closer to him since he's footing the bill.

When Stace says her line about how she knows me, how she knows I'm not like the characters I play on TV, time and time again, I feel the hair on my arms stand on end and the black of every night casts shadows across the sidewalk where I live, and makes the cats in the windows arch their backs.

* * *

I'm on location now, late February, filming my shooting scene when I get the call. It's really a message to call my agent, Bar Hendriks. My mind starts to unwind again and I become Clarence Judkins, scourge of the north forest. In the town of Harbor Cove I'm the one you can get drugs from. The show's supposed to be a cross between Melrose Place and Breaking Bad (with a little Dukes of Hazzard thrown in for the hell of it), but done straight (the PR people actually say that). The nicotine-thin actress from Malibu, with the red hair all teenage girls across the country are trying to copy, starts screaming a high-pitched falsetto torch-burning squeal, and it's my turn to howl and give some feeling to my next line: "Kelly, you should've done what I told you. No one looks in the trunk of my car." She's better now—her face a mask of determination—this actress, as she twirls and puts the kitchen table between us and pulls a gun out of her purse, which, coincidently, just happens to be left open and on the counter. We're in the moment; I don't even notice the room filled with cameras, men holding boom mikes, make-up workers over at the craft table stuffing their faces.

"I'll shoot you, Clarence. I don't want to, but I will," Kelly says. Her secret lover crashes into the room, takes the gun out of her hands, and says, "No you won't, baby, I will." And he does, and I want to laugh at whoever wrote their lines. Why wouldn't she want to shoot me? I've hit her more times than she can count. She avoids me when we're off camera lounging around. I gave her character two black eyes she hid from her Aunt, the old bitch who was against our marriage from the start of the season premiere, and the same high-society tramp who told Kelly she was disinherited as long as she stayed married to me; no more summer home in Charlevoix, Kelly.

Stace rubs my neck when I get back to the hotel where the cast and crew reside. The show provides cheap lodging in the hotel we use occasionally on camera in exchange for advertising. Stace is here for a week's vacation. She's a stuntwoman for hire but wants to go back to finish school for an architecture degree. Her father says he'll pay her way if she'll only postpone our wedding—forever. She stopped school the first time when she fell for a stuntman who convinced her she'd be perfect because she so closely resembled a flavor-of-the-moment starlet and she could work as much as she wanted. Off to stunt school; her daddy paid for that too.

"Thanks," I say.

"For what?"

"For getting the kinks out of my sore neck. That's where I carry all of my tension."

She's always questioning my graciousness. Sometimes I can't even be nice when I want to. Sometimes I feel like I'm going to be stuck playing the joker on every new show and movie from now until I rest in my grave. I really don't mind though. Sometimes Stace tells me she knows someone who could change my appearance within a month; make me look less intimidating and more heroic—she can introduce me to a personal trainer who once worked with Arnold back when he had muscle definition. "You could be the next Indiana Jones if you lifted weights, got a decent haircut, and ate sensibly," she says.

"I'm not going to change." There's no room to argue with me anymore even if I know that's what I want to do.

I say, "Bar called and told me he has an opening for me in a new horror film. He said I'd be paid double scale and time and a half for the hours it'll take to get me through makeup each day."

"No one will even know who you are underneath all that monster gear. You need to cultivate a recognizable face. I know someone who can redo your headshots. I'm only saying this to help you. My friend Erica redesigns stale websites and says she's willing to help you with an update."

"Stace. I'm kind of busy filming everyday. When could I find the time to do everything you want me to do?" I do stop short of sounding too resentful, but she takes my words as another link to what she views as my lack of ambition and far from what Stace wants to hear. She says, "You never listen to me!" Then she turns and closes the door behind her, but not like an actress would. She did leave with the dark brown plastic ice bucket and I have bottles of Irish whiskey and Pinot Grigio for her, the only thing Stace drinks. I know that much. I also know she'll come back soon enough, bounding onto the king-size bed right next to me as if we didn't just argue about stupid stuff, and kiss me, laugh, cajole some more, drink, watch a rerun and then fall off to sleep after we cuddle some more, but I won't ask if she wants to have sex because her leaving the room after telling me I never listen to her was really her answer to that question.

In an instant I'm thinking about my front stoop back in California; how warm it would be sitting in the dark and watching the feral cats creeping along the roofline. John, my neighbor from two apartments down, would be going out dressed in expensive suits and carrying his camera to take pictures at the latest art opening. I'd wish him a good night and he'd ask me if I wanted to join him. When I'd tell him no, maybe next time, he'd leave and L.A. night would come fast there and have me covered. The lights from the city would filter down and add a purplish bruised haze to the blackness. I'd open the black case beside me, the new one with the Rolling Turks' name on the front lid, and take out my gleaming sax. A slow grind of notes would place me in the sky; the noise of cars on endless highway systems would blend the rhythm until I had a chorus, and the smog would part like a stage curtain and let me into the darkness. Then my neighbor, Mrs. Rashly, would open her door, step out in her faded green slippers and matching caftan, and tell me to cut it out. She'd give me the eye of the weary. I should know better. The air around the apartment complex is communal space. Mrs. Rashly has already brought up my saxophone playing at the housing meetings. Someone sent me an official letter telling me the hours I could practice, and that I'd have to honor this request, play indoors.

I used to be pretty good on the sax, part of a band ever since my teen years, but I don't have time to keep it up. It's strictly one of those lost hobbies, and hardly soothing anymore

* * *

I don't have any lines now. Kelly's lover shot me and the bullet cut my speech function—again, writers, taking the lazy route. She and her lover, a richer and more striking hero-type, took me to the emergency room and dropped me off outside in the freezing cold. Stage blood dripped down from my chin onto the pavement while two actors, local extras, hoisted me onto a rolling stretcher and called for the trauma unit. "Dr. Mullit's on the way," a nurse screamed, one of the other pretty actresses who would soon fall for me while I recovered, and eventually help plot my revenge. This actress at least hid her cigarette addiction, I never saw her smoke, but all the gum in the world couldn't mask her bent breath as she hovered over my mute body, whispered into my character's bandaged ear.

Stace wants to go back to Corona and help her mother with the wedding plans. I told her that would be nice, and drove her to the Pellston airport where she'd catch her flight to Chicago and on to LAX. "I'll call you when I get there. Be a good boy."

Somehow I feel relief and not about the show and my acting, which is making a statement; the local newspaper's entertainment reporter, who also doubles for the lead sports writer and alternate feature editorial journalist, wrote an article about the suppressed violent nature of a percentage of people living in the secluded areas surrounding Traverse City and further north in the hunting woods of the Upper Peninsula. "We're sitting on a time bomb. Every year someone shoots someone else for no reason at all. Some say it's the snow, the fever of being so alone. On the highly acclaimed television series, "Harbor Cove," the character, Clarence Judkins, is a perfect example of this tinderbox condition. He lives with this terrible spark first hand: violence spurred on by environmental changes." I don't know what to think of that, but I like what the clip will do for me. It isn't a magazine cover, but people will look at me and wonder if I really act like Clarence in my off time.

Now that Stace is gone I don't have anyone to tell me how to change. The other cast members stay in rooms up and down the same wing where my corner bungalow is located between the maid's closet and a picture window looking out to the main parking lot. The others leave me alone for some reason. It's like I have a disease, and they don't want to get near me because they're too stupid to know I'm not contagious even when talking to me up close. I always become an outcast on any set. Heroes don't mingle with villains.

When I was filming Coma Man, the other actors would turn and walk another route if they saw me coming. I'm not treated right either; the writers always make me jump into slime or eat food made to look like something from a compost. People still think I'm going to hurt someone or knife the screenwriter. On the last day of filming a short-lived vampire series, I pulled out a rubber machete and raged, spittle flying out of my mouth, at the director, "I'm not gonna take your shit anymore." Just for that one split second, the best moment of any practical joke, they thought I'd gone crazy. The look on all the faces, the cameraman, story consultant, best boy, made me think of monkeys and the way their faces change in their cages when bad seeds start throwing pebbles at them from safely behind the bars. I laughed and bent the knife to show them it was only rubber—see? Only a joke. I never talked to that director again, but I laughed even more when I got back to my apartment and told Stace what happened.

"You keep doing things like that and you'll never get better scripts. You'll get a rep for being trouble and no one'll want to see you. Even to try out." I couldn't stop laughing and she went on, "And then where will you be? Not an actor. That's for sure."

She raised her hands to her hair, brown as rich dirt, and pulled it into a knot with quick knifing motions. Her arms looked like they were creating origami animals—vulnerable and sexy as hell. The next moment I'd pulled her into my arms and was hugging her so tight we both lost our breath. Stace giggled.

The darkness of Michigan brings me to the present situation. A lot of the younger starlets are down in Billy's hotel room killing time. He plays the young lover in the series, the guy who came to my wife's rescue and then dumped me cold at the hospital. I knew he was in for a fall when I recovered, even if he was an "upstanding" citizen of Harbor Cove. Kelly's Aunt, bless her heart, didn't approve of him either, and would come to me and the sweet nurse with plans to get rid of him. The Aunt is one of those crusty character actresses, been in the biz for decades, her weathered face instantly recognizable, and she's one of the few who survived the sinking of the Titanic in the movie Titanic. I watched that again just to spot her faked shivering in one of the half-full lifeboats, her hair straggly wet, the look of horror in her brilliant dark eyes. She could play the upper-crust leader of a well-to-do family in her sleep by now, and in this fading series, even she was phoning her performance in (at this point the director just moved onto the next scene, hardly had the will to make people shoot too many time-draining takes). The script had me taking her money and buying airline tickets to Jamaica, but one of the writers had thrown in this Mystic Cross business so I didn't know if things were going to change or not. Billy and the rest were partying in his room because he could get as much coke as he pleased, even up here where you'd think the people thought drugs stayed in Detroit. I'm not into that, and I had this itch to call some country policeman and make his day by snitching on young Billy of the heroic looks. That would make the local entertainment reporter's day. He'd think Christmas came early.

Santa Monica is where I stay when I'm blue. I play my sax indoors now (softly—soft enough so Mrs. Rashly can't hear me) and afterwards I sit on my stoop and imagine the notes washing out the sound of televisions and neighbors talking about what they did all day, or arguing about the life they lead and when things were going to change for the better. Most of the cats in the neighborhood slinking through the locked gates of the apartment complex are strays, and all of us residents banded together to adopt them, bought flea collars for them, and split the vet costs for neutering, rabies and distemper vaccinations. Mrs. Rashly leads the cat brigade, takes them in to get fixed, or to buy ear mite salve. Some in the complex can't or won't pay, but very few, and others give more so the cost of helping all these stray cats evens out. It's not much. Technically, the landlord doesn't allow pets in his apartments, but everyone keeps their doors open a crack during the day, even the grim-faced misanthrope with the unfortunate name of Garter Binks in the corner unit; most also leave bowls of water and dry cat food on their stoops for the pussycats when they're hungry. I even keep a litter box if they want to stay in at night or during the rainy season. The landlord knows all but turns a blind eye and wouldn't think of complaining. Mrs. Rashly would raise such a fuss if he ever mentioned the animal rule to her, and I don't keep them in that often. John calls the big, orange tomcat Bully because he's the only one who still has his balls. I call him Mr. Righteous and tell him he's the next on the chopping block and to get his kicks in while the getting's good. A mother cat with long silky white hair slinks along the rooftops and hangs out in the sunshine. I call her Zsa Zsa, but most of the others call her Miss Fluffy. The last regular stray is the only kitten to survive after Mr. Righteous and Zsa Zsa made it one night. I call him Jazz Hands, which makes Stace laugh. When I play my music he comes inside and rubs up against my legs, flops over onto his back and extends his jazz hands and I know I never want to leave this place.

* * *

Corinne, the nurse who loved me at first sight, is rubbing the hair on my chest, when this week's director yells, "Cut." He's a small, wiry man from Memphis who made it big shooting a couple videos for somber country singers. This is his first real chance at making a name for himself. In the beginning few days he was supposed to bring an added sensual gloom to the show. I could only think: Really? Where did they find him? He looked wet behind the ears, and I knew he'd be directing in the Hollywood machine for decades to come, and I imagined him aged and stooped behind his camera, croaking out his directions.

"I want some steamy heat here, folks. I want to test the limits of every censor out in Michelle Bachman country." I'm supposed to be recovering from a voice-stealing gunshot wound; supposed to be one step from dead; supposed to be making love to a fanatically "in love" nurse while bandages fly and the hospital bed, in the semi-private room, squeals and begins to rise and lower with no one touching the controls; supposed to hide my yelps of pleasure from the prim Harbor Cove librarian in the next bed, he who broke a couple ribs and his left leg falling down the library steps. The writers are going to make his part a bit larger, and try to make everyone believe he knows the secret location of the Copper Culture Tribe's ancient burial mound, where the Mystic Cross will grant anyone who finds it wealth and power. Like I'm going to believe some wingnut was pushed down the library's steps because he knew too much—right. The writing's getting a bit thin now, and the director wants Corinne and I to retake our positions.

"More lipstick kisses on his face, Corinne, and you guys? Try to keep the camera off his chest. All that hair makes him look like he's wearing a goddamn bathmat. Let's roll 'em, folks."

The tension in my neck grows so much the local doctor tells me I may have pinched a nerve there. "Your vertebrae are being pressed in by the muscle. I'll give you a prescription for a drug that should reduce the swelling." He doesn't tell me the name of this new wonder drug, but, in my pained, glowering silence, he grows nervous and says, "If it doesn't work we can try many others." I smile like a man capable of doing damage, and thank him (but I can't twist his head off later for prescribing $300 drugs that won't last a month if I take the three a day schedule clearly printed on the label). I swallow the pills and my neck feels fine; I can rotate my head with no pain. Stace calls wishing she could rub my worries and aches away. I tell her I can't talk long. She tells me she misses me. I say I hope her parents are doing well and she says she has to go, that mother wants to go to Fashion Island to buy her some new clothes and eat diet California pizza.

The Michigan snow is blowing up a howl and the cars in the parking lot are covered. In the morning, a bunch of us will carpool to the site and start the morning's breakfast scene. It's a common moment of every episode, where almost all the actors and actresses are getting ready for work or school or calling each other with their plans for the day. I'm supposed to get my first visit from Kelly's evil mother tomorrow. She'll talk to me while Corinne, my nurse of the fawning eyes, answers for me or translates my nods and grunts. A couple times I'll speak out loud and make the director re-shoot the scene: just to make trouble, and make him think about going back to Memphis. Whoever heard of shooting a love scene in a semi-private hospital room, making faked love on a haunted bed that runs of its own accord? It was the director's idea. I'm supposed to be in pain here.

* * *

Later in the evening, Ruba Leesh, who plays Corinne, the sex-crazed nurse in all my scenes from now on, knocks on my hotel room door, pops her pretty almond-shaped head in and asks me if I want to order dinner from the hotel's crappy planked whitefish restaurant. She and a couple of the crew are going to bring the food back to her room and watch the show, one of the early episodes we filmed last April. I decline and wish her a good night. I find it hard to believe she's even bothering with me.

Ruba says, "You know, you don't have to live like your character. We like you." I hold my breath. "You're not so bad, Clarence. See you tomorrow." Then the door's closed and I'm left wondering if she even knows my real name. And why wouldn't she use it if she's trying to tell me I don't have to be Clarence?

My father was an actor signed by a studio in the fifties for any part suitable. He usually played the sidekicks of the good guys. He was shorter than most and had an interesting face: a straight nose over full lips and a strong jaw. The studio owned him and made him act in a lot of forgettable films, but he was good and wouldn't stop trying because he loved the life. When I told him I wanted to be an actor he gave me a hug and introduced me to a producer he'd been friendly with for decades. My father made everything look easy even though he wasn't leading man material. He was never out of work and lived a good life. When he died last year I missed not telling him he was my inspiration and my favorite character actor. Stace tried to comfort me as much as she could. She held my hand during the funeral.

* * *

This time I'm falling. Corinne (Ruba Leesh) and I are driving in the black Pontiac, going fast on the icy bluff road, trying to outrun the police, the librarian in the leg cast, and a string of other townspeople. We just stole the Mystic Cross from Kelly and Kelly's double-crossing mother. They were in cahoots all along, getting close to men who could help them find the burial mound.

Before the action started, the director said to me, "In this scene you'll want to show you're still tough. No one to be fooled with.

You have to get away. You don't even care about Corinne next to you and you'll want to be driving like a madman." He smiled because he knew this was my death scene, and I wouldn't be around anymore to cause trouble.

"No problem," I said.

The curve comes from nowhere and the car crashes through the guardrail. Before the car falls two hundred feet to the rocks and deep water below, where the Mystic Cross will remain lost; before I see the curve and start wishing I was handsome and playing the local rock of Harbor Cove, Sheriff Carter, I turn to Corinne and say my last line, "Hold on tight, Honey, we'll play through this hole." I didn't know who wrote my lines, but I tried to sound menacing and true to my character. Clarence, as far as I could tell, never liked golf, and only played it with Harbor Cove's elite to curry favor. The writers and the know-it-all director couldn't see that my character wouldn't be caught dead on a golf course, and they somehow forgot that with my gunshot throat wound still raw, unhealed, I wouldn't be able to even say my last line—bozos.

The car crashes and I'm out of the series. Stace is surprised to see me when I fly home to Santa Monica. I tell her we wrapped up my last episode faster than expected and here I am.

"Are you going to take that part in the horror film?" she asks.

"Probably," I say. I want to hold her and let her change my mind, but I can't walk over to her.

"I have to go back home for awhile and prepare for the GRE and fill out applications." She fiddles with her fingernails, and almost brings them up to her face so she can bite them. I know she's trying to quit biting them, and I know I don't want to see her again. If I say anything she'll tell me I'm being true to my character. So I don't say a word when she kisses my cheek and leaves.

When July comes hotter than a bonfire, the city seems to sleep during the day. No one walks in front of my apartment except John. Everyone else is on vacation. I'm resting my neck, which is now a dull ache, before I head for the beach. On my way over I'm supposed to make a detour to the studio to go over the script. I was picked to play a reptilian creature hatched from an alien egg; and found by another fame-seeking teenage boy, who gets his girlfriend to help him open it. They do and spend the rest of the movie running from me.

Someone I don't know steps in front of my door and crouches down. I can see him petting Zsa Zsa and making soft appraisals. I open the screen door slowly and tell him, "That's the momma cat."

"She's great," he says. He looks up at me, smiles and says, "I liked your show. You were really good."

I don't know what to think, but I reply, "Thanks. It wasn't anything special."

"I'm staying with John for a couple days. On vacation from Michigan." His skin is a light tan color, and will probably burn here in the pale but hot sun.

"It's pretty nice out there now." I can talk about weather with the best of people.

He scratches Zsa Zsa's ears and says, "John told me all about the cats around here." He seems nervous. His arms are swinging in front of him until he brings them up to his chest and holds them.

I want to know if he's nervous because he's in front of an actor, a real-life, dime-a-dozen celebrity, and doesn't want to impose on my precious time, or if my appearance, rough stubble in the morning, is sending warning signals to him.

"You have to see Mr. Righteous and Jazz Hands. They're family to Zsa Zsa." I can't believe I'm talking cats with some guy from Michigan. "What's your name?" I say.

"Dave." He stands up all the way.

I stick out my hand and Dave shakes it once tightly and lets go. I say, "My name's Leo. Nice to meet you." Dave walks back to John's apartment and my screen door shuts after I rub Zsa Zsa's white belly.

Later that day, as the sun begins to crawl beneath the horizon line, I'm out on the front steps cleaning my sax (I'm not going to play it Mrs. Rashly—I stare at her window as she peeks out). The night's a humid mess and I want the darkness to fill me up. I call Stace's parents' house and her mother tells me she's out. She won't say where. I mumble goodbye and hang up. In a minute I'll belt out a wandering note so blue it'll start the cats howling and I'll watch them tear into each other, biting and clawing; defending their territory. I'll go inside and lock my door behind me.

* * *

When the morning lifts, and I begin to stir, usually around noon, I pack up and go to the beach a mile away from my apartment. I drive because I'm so used to it. Everyone drives here in L.A. even when only going two blocks. If I see people walking I think there's some big reason: car failure or accident. The sand is hot and my beach umbrella covers my body so I can sleep.

I play music most nights now (I have time to practice in a band mate's garage) and the Rolling Turks are starting to get a meager following. A few people have seen every show we've ever done. I talked to one of them and he said he hoped we never got so big we forgot about all our true fans, the ones who supported us from the very beginning. I said I hope so too, but I'm not sure he believed me. He thinks we're going to sell out like everyone else he's been disappointed with. I think I scared him away somehow. They keep coming back though. By the time I get home from a gig I sleep like the dead, drag myself to the beach and rest for the coming night.

My saxophone burns in my hands as I play an original riff and Jazz Hands curls at my feet; I know he's aware of the changing notes as I watch his tail twitch. When I stop playing Jazz Hands awakes and heads for the front door. I open it and go sit in front of my apartment door in a wooden chair. I wait there staring at nothing in the night sky.

John comes out of his apartment two doors down holding his camera and asks me where Stace has been. I tell him I don't know. Maybe doing more stunt work and trying to talk her way into school.

John says he's sorry and gently shrugs his shoulders and leans against the stair railing. He's a fine art photographer and computer genius. He was going to take the wedding pictures, as a friend to us, and I tell him we had to postpone. He says, "Sure, anytime though, okay? Count on me." He has too big a name now to photograph weddings anyway and was only going to bring his camera by request. When I moved to this neighborhood, he welcomed me in and gave me a framed photo he took of a beautiful Indian woman, short black hair parted in the middle, sitting in a wooden tub full of water. Her look was captured there and reflected by the pool of dark water: one of expectation and guilt. I told John he did good work and the woman's complex expression was striking.

John sits down in the chair next to me and I think back to Harbor Cove's season finale. The show wasn't being picked up for another year and I was secretly relieved. I didn't fawn around the other actors and movie people who had connections to bigger things. I liked where I was. I said to myself I was happy. Stace wanted to suspend the wedding. I said that would be okay. In two weeks she had all her stuff, the t-shirts with Stunt Woman across the front, the battered cowboy boots, the books rating the best architecture schools, and she was gone without a note.

I expected one, but I guess I don't know everything. The engagement ring I gave her six months ago rests in its black velvet box on the kitchen island.

John stays awhile even though we don't really strike up a conversation. He finally says he has a photo shoot. "Keep playing. I like it even if Lady Rashly doesn't," he says, and then leaves. Mr. Righteous shows up later but won't let me touch him. His left ear is bleeding, cut and in tatters, and I wonder what he did to deserve the pain. He hisses and looks so monstrous. I open my screen door and follow him inside so I can feed him and play my part.

Under the Third Story Window

Mrs. Applebaum throws the rubber ball, a toy of her son's, at Mr. Applebaum. It misses and sails out the open window. The boy squeals when he realizes his ball has flown away, is gone.

The small round shadow falls from the third story. Megan watches the rubber ball bounce down the front stoop steps and into 12th Street. She laughs and wants to get up and chase the glitter-speckled ball. It reminds her of the cheap toys her father bought for her when she was younger, twiddling impatiently in the grocery store aisle, darting off to pluck a big rubber super-ball from its wire tower, and bring it back with hopeful eyes.

She said, "This one for me, Papa?" Unsure, but precocious, and her papa found himself unable to refuse.

Two kids dash across to Block's Market. One of them pockets shiny apples and eats grapes while the other distracts the porky grocer with a question about cigarette prices. Megan watches them and tries to hide in the shadow of the steps with her face slanting down, becoming rounded chin and willowing hair. Last week, they took her along when they went to explore the Forster Building before it was demolished. The city is refurbishing, trying to come out of its shell a bit by exploding the old landmarks, the old tenements in disrepair to make room for fancier, taller, baby boomer condos, the beginning of a gentrification phase. One of the boys is named Stu, and the other is his leader, Carmichael. When Megan followed them into the building, she knew what all of them were going to do before they did it, and she doesn't know why she felt so free. If they see her, they'll want to do it again, and she doesn't feel like it.

A Greek, wearing light tweed, owner of Prizzo Printing passes Megan's stoop and she raises her red skirt, gives him a peek and giggles as the Greek turns beet faced and hurries on. Easy enough. The exhibitionist in her calls to her to get up and run after the man, show him what is there, let him touch it. This is the way the world turns, Megan believes.

A yellow taxi cruises by and hits the rubber ball so it rolls into a drain. Megan gives the cabdriver the finger. The cabdriver squeals his tires and shouts out, "Lousy whore." Megan's smile vanishes. It is where she is, dressed for the heat in strips to cool off. The place her parents left for her. The place she was raised. She waits for Momma to come home, late, when dogs scatter across the back, vacant parking lots, barbed wire fences surrounding them. She waits to make sure she is safe, to hear her mother come in the door and talk to her about Mrs. Gartenburken, the office gossip, who goes into the supply room with any man who breathes oxygen. The hospital is overrun with her kind. Megan wonders if Momma ever did anything like Mrs. Gartenburken; Momma is alone now. They both are, and they're both lonely. When Momma asks Megan if she looked for a job today, Megan will say she stood in line at unemployment for hours and they closed by the time the counter reached her, close enough to touch.

Another shadow, this one larger, flops from the same third story window. Megan winces as the boogie-box shatters on the pavement in front of her. Toby, the boy in the room, still bawls and Megan hears him try to separate his parents. Mr. Applebaum tells him to get lost. She hears a smack. The music in the music box quits with a squawk. A Duracell rolls out of the mess and follows the rubber ball. Megan wonders if she should move across the street, out of firing range. All the Applebaums are causing a racket, something better than television, something real, where the outcome is unknown, unpredictable and would draw huge ratings if it wasn't real, if it played like a crime drama on the boob tube. It's almost as if she can feel it in the air. Megan thinks about the neighborhood and everyone on the sidewalk ready to spring, pop with anticipation. Usually someone calls. A police car, lights blazing, comes scurrying; the policemen get out all business and scared, sweat a veil across their faces; they think everyone is a psychopath, even the paraplegic across the street, Rufus, who played the best neighborhood b-ball until a drive-by stray bullet entered his spine, is a wacko because he scowls and curses at everyone who looks his way. Usually it's Myrna Trapsalli, the old woman on four, who lives above the Applebaums, who rings the police and tattles to them about all domestic disturbances. It's a common thing in this neighborhood. The heat, the haze, the motion of people on the street, the sly look of the business owners giving everyone the once-over, contributes to everything that's wrong in this country as far as Megan is concerned. She twists her hair into a curl with a finger and glances to her left, where the sun seems to rest on top of a skyscraper far, far away, red, haunting, a ball of raw anger loose among the people.

The lesbians from the corner brownstone stroll by holding hands. The one who looks like Barbara Walters gives Megan a glance and clutches her lover's hand tighter. The one who resembles Bridget Bardot also gives Megan a keen look. Megan raises her skirt, lets Bardot have a peek and giggles as Walters yanks her open-mouthed friend away.

An emaciated black boy, who sleeps in a derelict car raised up on cement blocks in the alley between Block's Market and the newer, gray high-rise, picks at the remains of the boogie-box. He grabs the slightly bent antenna. After running up the steps, the boy stops and bows in front of Megan and knights her with an antenna-tap to the shoulder. Smiling gravely, teeth protruding from under his upper lip, the alley boy skitters away with his treasure tucked inside his brown sweatshirt. He also stops in front of Rufus and shows him the antenna, knights him too, and then vanishes down the alley. Rufus's face becomes blank, an etching of happiness avoided until he stares right at Megan and curves away when she smiles at him. He raises a fist high above his head as if mocking her and solidarity. Megan can hear the wheels in his old chair creaking with rust as he turns himself left to watch the sun hit the buildings like daggers.

The newly knighted Megan runs her small hands through her charcoal hair again and starts braiding. An ambulance whizzes by, bathing her in red light for an instant. Megan gives the ambulance driver the finger, but he doesn't react, and she resolves to give him the finger before he passes next time, so she is noticed.

Megan's father's been taken and locked away five years ago after Momma walked in quietly to say goodnight, startled herself when she saw Megan's eyes, the lack of understanding, the questioning why, when she saw Papa fumbling in the dark, and sneaking up behind him to make sure he'd never do it again. The police came and carted him off. Papa was rubbing his head, and his last words to Momma were, "Why'd you have to hit me so hard?" Megan's mother works for the hospital on 10th Street as a receptionist in the Pulmonary Clinic. It's an honest job, she always told Megan and Papa, when he was still around. Who makes the money in this house? Momma hangs this over Megan's head every time they speak, but Megan knows she likes to keep it that way, to feel superior, and to keep her only child home, to make sure she's still safe, to fend off loneliness.

Megan hears a shriek and twists her head up to see Mrs. Applebaum flung out the third story window. She does a flip and meets Myrna Trapsalli's Plymouth Fury with a bone-crunching thump.

Megan listens as Mr. Applebaum shouts, "You BITCH." Their little boy is howling. "You want some more now?" The boy becomes silent.

Megan stares at the Plymouth's new hood ornament, wondering about the broken windshield-wipers that now point at the cloudless sky. This is only the beginning, Megan thinks.

The neighborhood gathers.

The alley boy returns long enough to nab the Plymouth's radio antenna from where Mrs. Applebaum's crash has snapped it onto the sidewalk, and then rushes back home. Megan starts to feel her control slipping away. The cement under her grows colder in the heat somehow and the faces of the staring neighbors stretch and distort like carnival clowns. This is the world turning slowly, watching what people do with a microscope, and fathoming nothing from the wreckage, not even what's buried in the rubble. Megan begins to stand up, to back away and turn inside, follow the dark hall to her small apartment she used to share with both her parents, father and mother, but she lowers herself and remains in place, a witness to the event, the only one who knows why people do the things they do. She can hear her mother at night asking her what she does all day, with all the time on her hands, do you even look for a job, and the sound of crying and praying and the sighing snores of bitter sleep. Look what I do for you.

Policemen come with the med unit and enter the building, passing Megan on their way up the front steps.

The last policeman in the row stops on the top riser and says in a gruff voice, "You people back away from here. This ain't no movie." He looks like an old war statue.

When he turns his back and moves into her building, Megan almost shouts, 'Fuck you', but catches herself because she wishes she was a policeman so she could capture Mr. Applebaum and rough him up a little with some police brutality. Mr. Applebaum never turns red-faced and never looks away when she lets him see what's under her skirt, and Megan hates him for it. She's stopped showing him, and now it's taken out of her hands.

The police shove Mr. Applebaum, who is bleeding from a gash in his left cheek, down Megan's steps and lock him in a blue-lighted squad car. Another policeman holds the little Applebaum boy by the hand and coos to him like he's a pigeon, someone to be fed and then shooed away when he gets too messy. He's placed in another car and his little moon-colored face peeks out the window, drowning in red light. All Megan catches is the blankness there, his face a wash of emotion and misunderstanding. The med boys heft Mrs. Applebaum up, zip her into a black bag and drive away, leaving hopscotch chalk, metal, glass, gutter leaves, grass, and weeds growing in the sidewalk cracks.

Rufus wheels away from the wreck shaking his head as if he's God saying I told you so.

Myrna Trapsalli squeaks, "Who gonna fix my car? Who gonna do that?" She squints at Megan, and Megan shrugs her shoulders.

The crowd disperses. Myrna sighs and limps back to the fourth floor wishing she had called the cops sooner. She'll never find replacement parts for her old relic of an automobile. The sun travels further west.

The two apple thieves run past Megan and give her the finger. Megan starts to cry and shakes a fist at them. She doesn't know what's wrong with her. It's her Papa. He's gone now, sent away for years because they said he was messed up in the head. No one is supposed to make her cry.

Carmichael and Stu stop running and saunter back over to her steps, the front entrance, and leer down at her. "Is your Momma home?"

Megan's quick with her response, no nonsense. "No, so why don't you fuck off." She stares into Stu's eyes, and makes him glance down at his beat-up, unlaced high-tops. Then she focuses her fury on Carmichael's gray irises, as if she can shoot beams of destruction from the red sun. The instant picture comes to mind: in the Forster building with them leading her up, up to the second story.

Carmichael chuckles and leers and says, "We were hoping you'd help us with that," and they both laugh some more like backwoods gas station attendants.

Megan watches the picture unroll in front of her like film in a broken machine. The image of her held down on the floor by the boys so keen on trying to be men, calling her names: whore, slut, father-fucker, saying she likes it, asking her what her father did to her, and why he was sent away, and wasn't it all her fault? The image flips to her Papa, five years before, entering her bedroom and touching her and telling her it's all right, don't worry, this won't hurt, the smell of alcohol and cigarettes, touching her breasts, their newness, what he'd been noticing, watching them grow. And Momma descends. Now, the boys say, "Who you going to tell? Do you think anyone will believe someone like you? You're old enough. We'll tell everyone you corrupted us."

They howl with laughter and slap palms when Megan starts to cry more. "We'll be watching you, baby." Carmichael drawls. "We'll come get you when they're ready to bomb another building. We'll make our own explosions." They leave, sauntering down the sidewalk as if their number will never be called.

Megan loves it when people stop to talk with her, when they never fight back.

She remembers one man who did more than stop. He asked her why she looked so sad, sat next to her and put his arm around her shoulders as he lead her to his car.

But Megan's tired and the memory burns, so she stands up, stretches like a cat, turns, and walks into the apartment building.

She'll come back out when it's dark to wait for her mother to come home, to watch the cars go by with night music blaring, to give someone a peek and laugh and laugh.

On the Back Staircase

The red farmhouse is dark. In one of the four upstairs bedrooms, Anna keeps waking up, restless, unnerved, making up stories in her head. God. It's so dark. And, finally, she can't bring herself back to sleep anymore. Is this one of those dreams where the dream is so real you wake up feeling like you've worn out the whole day already? Anna hopes not because this dream or this reality is scaring her.

Anna spent the last two hours lying on her bed, under two heavy blankets, staring out the cold, splintered casement window at the stars. By design, the window opened like a door right over the front porch roof; in case of fire, the family would escape with a ten-foot leap down to the ground, without thinking of broken ankles, legs, for very long, but Anna couldn't think of anything else. The stars in the chilly night sky moved, twirled into new shapes, like cloud watching after waking from a deep sleep when the clouds acted out your dreams.

Two hours ago Anna heard three locks fasten as the rest of her family went to sleep, her parents coming up last to make sure Jeff and Alan were really in their proper bunk beds and not throwing pillows at each other. The boys' door was locked from the inside; no fighting sounds could be heard so Anna's parents brushed their teeth, alternating spits of Crest into the shell-shaped basin.

Her parents always end up doing their nightly rituals together. They are never apart, as if they are the twins. They even teach art at the same university, and share a large painting studio.

After switching the bathroom nightlight on, which gave off a warm condensed-orange glow, Anna's parents shuffled into their bedroom down the hall. Anna heard their slide-bolt click and a spontaneous burst of laughter from Mom, then, distinct, even if a bit hushed: "There's a rip in your boxer shorts." Anna pictured Mom getting a needle and thread and fixing the tear while Dad still wore them. She knew that wouldn't happen and Anna listened intently to more giggling, and an hour later, light snoring.

The walls in the old, barn red, Victorian, rambling, 1895 farmhouse are thin. It's 1981, and Anna wonders if they'll give their home a centennial birthday celebration, and then what the original family members who lived in the farmhouse were like.

A little while ago Anna saw something outside on the rural highway, large and slow moving. It started walking up the driveway, but then it vanished. One second it was there, a man-like form outlined against the whitewood fence separating Anna's house from her neighbors', The Smith's, modern ranch house, and the next second it's gone.

She knows she can't sleep now. She won't, even if she closes her eyes. Anna thinks: I'll keep watch. She imagines the dark man of shadow breaking in and slipping along the cool brown-tile flooring of the kitchen, slowly sliding a knife, the one used to slice onions and bagels, out of the creaky drawer, and she listens for that creak.

Anna's so sure he's there that she scolds herself for scaring herself with her dreams, but, she thinks: what if there is a murderer down in the kitchen right now making plans? Who to kill first, whom to kill last, whom to make scream the longest. What will I do if he is skulking there? There's no lock on my door.

Maybe she should wake Dad to go check downstairs, but he has to teach his early class tomorrow, and it's almost 2:30 in the morning now. He'll be mad if this turns out to be another of Anna's late-night wolf cries. But then, he'll be mad if someone did break in, something he's always worrying about. Anna doesn't think her father could put up much of a fight against a maniac with dark ridges of muscle lining his forearms and chest; someone who stores up psychotic energy like a battery, who lives for destruction, a bloody rendering of the family unit, like the serial killer in that freaky new *Red Dragon* book her parents kept raving about and then tried to keep out of her naturally curious reach. Her parents loved scary books too. Anna had to sneak the Harris novel out of her parents' room to read little by little, captivated as she learned about the psycho who worked in a film development plant and chose his victims, entire families, by poring over their everyday birthday, Easter Sunday dinner, vacation photos: apple-pie families on picnics, brothers playing catch, sister and mother helping each other set the table for a special celebration dinner, father holding the new baby, staring into the camera, into the eyes of the killer.

Dad keeps telling his family: "The deadbolt on the front door is so flimsy, Ruby could've broken it down."

They reply: "Ruby's dead," which would stymie the conversation, but do nothing about fortifying the front door. Ruby was the first family pet, an old border collie mix who got hit by a car down the road a bit two years ago, but Dad would always bring her up when the family was all together in the same room because she hadn't been replaced yet.

Anna hopes her Dad wants a new pet for Christmas.

As Anna gazes at a dim star, she knows, deep down inside, she hasn't really heard anyone moving around downstairs, and she's wondering if she did see someone vanish on the gravel driveway. It could've been a cloud covering the sliver moon, a wind whipping October leaves into the bushes, maybe, but she also believes, down so deep now—I saw it—and she scolds herself anew—the shadow moving like an arm swinging by someone's side, someone strong, and muscled, and dark, clothes the color of night.

The star that barely blinks light reminds Anna of the orange bathroom nightlight one unlocked door away. Alan usually gets up in the middle of the night, stumbles to the bathroom, and forgets to flush, not because he's half awake but because he always forgets. Dad hung a hand-painted sign on the bathroom door that reads: FLUSH FOR LIFE—as if the next time Alan forgets, he'll have no future and end up cleaning the bathroom for the rest of his life.

Turning into the kitchen, right near the back wall and the old white floor freezer, are the first steps of the back staircase. There are five steps, worn oak, taking you to a landing, a dark wider square space. The rest of the staircase steps branch to the left and lead you further, up twenty-one steep steps to the second floor landing. These wooden steps are painted eggshell blue to make the dark corridor lighter, but the color doesn't help brighten anything; the blue takes the light in, stores it up and makes Anna run down the stairs faster or take the front staircase.

After the man gets his knife and adds it to his darkening form he'll head for the first step, but he'll do it in his shadowy and sneaky way because Anna thinks he is aware now that someone upstairs is aware of him. He wants to do things carefully, make no mistakes.

The back staircase is next to the bathroom door, to the left once you reach the landing, and Anna's door is down from that maybe only ten feet at the turn in the corridor, which means Anna's bedroom door faces the back stairs. Before Dad bought the nightlight for the bathroom, Alan, sleepwalking, wandered out his bedroom door, to the right of the back staircase, and opposite the bathroom door. If this sounds confusing, try juggling for bathroom rights on every school day. Anna always beats her sisters into the shower, and they usually scream for Mom to get her to hurry up. Anyway, Alan walked out his door and must've thought he was going into the bathroom when, in fact, he was walking out into thin air. He fell down the slippery, painted, back staircase and broke his right leg in two places. Anna found him first, lying on the landing, because she always wakes up fast. Alan screamed there, injured and afraid of what happened and what was to come. Mom cried with him. Megan sat next to Jeff and Sandy, huddled at the top of the stairs.

Dad said, "Anna, go call an ambulance, dial 911." So she did, feeling pretty important. Alan's back was twisted in a funny position and Dad didn't want to chance moving Alan himself. Anna will always remember how her brother's face was lit up by scream after scream. By the time Alan came back home with a cast from thigh to ankle on his right leg, there was a nightlight in the upstairs bathroom. A cloud covers the star Anna's watching and she focuses on another, brighter one.

Then she hears . . .

A creak on the back staircase, and it's a sly one, as if someone's trying to sneak up, as if that someone wants Anna to hear that old creak. Or is it just the house settling? Thin walls? Either way, Anna won't go check and she thinks: Oh my God—anyway. Why do I insist on scaring myself?

Anna's twin sister, Sandy, the one she shares a room with, is asleep on the other twin bed across the bedroom, tucked under covers in the darkness. Anna says softly, "I heard something. Sandy, are you awake?"

Sandy only mumbles, "Shut up," and falls back into slumber. Anna is amazed at how quickly her sister departs to dreamland, as if a switch is flipped.

Anna thinks about the design of the house, wondering, keeping in mind the subtle shifting of weight she thinks she heard on the first wooden step. There are two staircases in the house. The first and main front staircase is covered with an old family runner, blood red, blue, aged-bone oriental carpet and the secondary back staircase, starting near the kitchen counter island, ancient wood. No one can ever sneak up on anyone, Anna, Sandy, Jeff, Alan, or Megan, using the back stairs. They can never sneak up on their parents, when they're cooking meals, either, but they do keep trying. They're a family made up of sneaks. All five kids are just at those ages, all of them yet to cross into their teenage years, but Megan's only a month away, and Sandy and Anna turn twelve in nine months.

Anna wants to remember, or keep it in mind, that her family locks their bedroom doors when they go to sleep. Everyone except Sandy and Anna, who, out of sheer laziness, opted not to install a lock of their own; Anna feels that no one in her family is safe anymore, tonight. It's so late now and the moon has spun farther away, deepening the blackness of the driveway, where she wouldn't see any shadow if it moved.

There's no lock on Anna's bedroom door. Sandy and Anna don't have an inside lock, a slide-bolt, or chain.

Once, Anna walked into the television room and asked for a simple hook and clasp: "Everyone else has one." But she didn't push for it.

Dad replied, not even listening to Anna completely, watching a PBS show with lots of poor static reception, "You'll have to install it yourself."

Anna's a very lazy person. She won't even clean her half of the room unless an extreme threat or blackmail is involved. Anna never thought she had a reason to push for a lock. Sandy and I never needed one before, she thinks, and besides, I like it when Jeff and Alan barge in demanding attention, wanting to play board games.

The others all had their own reasons for locks.

Anna starts to play a mind game. Instead of counting sheep, she sits up in bed with her back against the simple pine headboard and convinces herself that on this weekend October night she's the only person awake in the house, the only night owl up near this house, the only sleepless creature on the rolling yard, outside the Ohio town limit, where the television cable stopped three hundred yards from their house, right on the corner, and wouldn't come no matter how many calls to the cable company went through— the roof antenna bringing in scratchy versions of the three big networks, in Granville proper, the small university town, no one on campus pulling all-nighters, everyone still asleep, but, when awake, the people bicker about how the college kids drink too much at the #1 party college in the nation and whiz through town without a care, knowing their parents are footing the bill for their games, in sleeping Licking county, a half-hour drive to Columbus, where Dad and Mom drive the family to Chess King Malls, the JCPenney outlet store, where all returned merchandise finds a home, and Schottenstein's to try on discount clothing for hours, in what the siblings call the silver cattle wagon, the youngest twins yearning to sit in the way back reverse bench seat so they can stare at the drivers of cars behind them and make funny faces, every weekend to escape the conservative, political, bureaucratic yammering of the school administrators. In the sleepy state of Ohio, where jobs have always been scarce and businesses think the state is made up of the finest cross-section of America and try to test their products here first before setting up nationwide, as if Ohioans like being guinea pigs, in the United States of America, where the President can fall down a lot and become the butt of jokes, and the next President can be a peanut farmer and become ridiculed for another reason, the new President elected, to Anna anyway, acting as if he'd just aced his session on a Hollywood casting couch; endlessly, in the Northern Hemisphere, Anna imagines a continent asleep, everyone lying on cots, in tents, on cold ground, in caves, and then around the world, where natural disasters are the only thing that binds the different, bickering countries with penny-can compassion, but Anna's mind tires of the game when she pictures the entire universe asleep and how a big bang would wake it up, and then she thinks about how dark the hallway outside her door is and about the two staircases and all the locks. She tries to listen to Sandy's breathing. The sound is cool and low like a breeze in a field. As she listens, Anna tries to catch the sound of breathing outside the door on the back staircase, but she can't focus enough to hear anything.

Megan sleeps in a room around the corner, down the same short hallway as their parents' room. With some relief, Anna ponders anew: if the man chose to kill the kids in order, Megan would be the first to go; she's the oldest. She has her own room. For privacy, Megan has an inner door lock. That is her reason. Once, Jeff crept in with a loaded crayon box and made his own celestial system, a purple, blue, orange and red galaxy, out of Megan's papers, books and posters. She needs the lock because of the door itself; it's warped badly and will never shut closed. Ruby would claw open Megan's door and hop onto her faded-rose comforter for a snooze, smelling up the room with dog. So a hook-lock was put on the outside also, and there are dog-clawing scratches as a

Ruby reminder. Alan locked Megan in once for four hours when their parents were away and Megan was supposed to be babysitting the lot. Alan was grounded for two weeks. But Megan's inner lock would surely break under the shadow-man's thrust. The door would splinter on its Sears hinges and he'd rush in, knife held ready to swing forward in a curve. Anna can see Megan opening her eyes and looking into the darkness where the man's features should be, being swallowed up by the fear, the arm arcing down, and the cold blade slicing through her comforter.

Anna blows the image to smithereens by thinking about her younger brothers, fraternal twins, Alan and Jeff, how little safety their door lock is, how they are so much alike even though they are so far from identical. The monstrous man on the stairs hasn't taken another step—who is testing the night air even now, making his plans, will take another step soon, and Anna's waiting for the next creak. Alan and Jeff should be able to hear him coming because their bedroom is closest, but they're sound asleep after a full evening of kick the can with the neighborhood kids.

Alan and Jeff work in tandem, one prank after another. Jeff is the youngest of the family, by barely ten minutes, Alan breathing air first and squalling, waiting for his twin's cries to join in a chorus. They also share a room, but they have a lock on their door because they both whined loudly when Megan got two locks. They have other reasons too. They feel their things, Tinker Toys and Lego sculptures and comic books, are more important then anyone else's possessions, and should be kept behind locked doors. They like to sneak around in order to intrude in their older siblings' affairs;

they have to be able to plan schemes behind closed doors. Sandy and Anna can't wait until they grow up, are constantly throwing the maturity word around when they learned it from Megan, when the boys will figure out how sloppy they are and clean up their act. With the lock issue, Dad put them on probation. If they abuse the lock on the door, he takes it off.

But they have a lock and because of that they are safe. Everyone would hear the man trying to break through their door, all the noise shooting throughout the house and walls, giving Mom enough time, even on the old black rotary phone in her bedroom, to call 911, while Dad rushes out into the hall to confront the intruder. Anna fears for him and keeps quiet. She thinks: what if the man went after my dad first? What if I had no parents? She wouldn't know what to do then so she's happy for her brothers' safety from the sounds and anything making sounds on the back staircase. She pulls the covers up to her chin and listens. She knows the house and can see blueprints as if they are veins running across the back of her hand, floor plans as if they are right in front of her, glowing.

Every room has its own smell and every room makes its own creaks. Sandy and Anna have talked about these sounds and how they can tell when someone is in another room by the tread on the floorboards in the dining room or the squeak on the tile in the kitchen. Sandy can tell someone is coming up the back staircase because, she says, the creak sounds like a swaying, snapped sail on a wind-tossed ship. Sandy and Anna share their mother's melodramatic streak.

Sandy and Anna are also fraternal twins. Sandy, with a small, rabbity nose, dimpled chin, straw-blonde hair, looks nothing like her twin sister, Anna, who has dark curls in her hair Mom tries to straighten by brushing the heck out of them, and wide brown eyes to match. They are both pretty, and look nothing like Megan, who has a smattering of freckles across her straight nose, and new braces.

"You'll get them too," said Megan, "just you wait."

Everyone Anna's talked to jokes about the two sets of twins some way or another as if they must feel sorry for poor, poor Mom because she was so busy changing diapers or changing something else, trying to pick up one child without making the other twin instantly jealous. They talk about how different all five children look, how three pregnancies brought five babies into this world looking like individuals and not clones. They are amazed by this and laugh about the three different postmen who delivered mail on their street. Anna thinks people have to be cruel at times to hide their own insecurities. She admits being guilty of this from time to time.

Sandy and Anna don't dress in the same clothes, the same color. Even when they were born, they were different. Sandy was larger, louder, almost resentful, with a sharp analytical mind, and Anna was the quiet one with the expansive fascination, the one who always wanted to know why, what, who, and where first before placing all of the real facts into an imaginary landscape?

Anna listens hard for any sound coming from out in the hall and down the back staircase and thinks of dark twins, the good and the bad and she wonders if the man on the stairs has the same purpose, if he's really a twin in search of his lost twin. That would mean he was looking for Megan, and that he wasn't really a man at all, just a dark boy on the teenage cusp, and the image of Megan's door exploding and Megan's twin rushing to join with her again in this world makes Anna shiver, and she tries to count down from ten to calm her nerves. Megan is safe, Anna thinks. She has to be. Anna can't hear anything from the back staircase. And she goes back to thinking the intruder is once again a man, a destructive force. It couldn't possibly be a twin, a long lost member of her family.

Megan wanted a twin. Anna always wondered if she felt left out because of not getting one, until the day when Mom told all the kids Megan showed some form of jealousy. Megan always protested mildly. You'll often find the family digging through their box of photographs. They didn't have an album. They had a large, sturdy, cardboard box. The photos Dad took are thrown in year after year and the box's corners are now taped together because it's handled so much.

A photo of Megan always surfaces; she's naked and splashing with glee in a yellow-duck-bordered baby pool in the early seventies, the sunlight shining in her eyes so no one can tell she has the darkest blue eyes of the family, as if they had been painted with three extra layers.

Everyone laughs as the picture is passed around. Megan was a pretty baby, is a pretty child, and she knows when she's center-stage and loves the role.

A similar photo was taken, two years later, of Sandy and Anna in the same duck pool, not as bright, the plastic wearing thin and mud-smudged. Anna swears she remembers the photo being taken—Dad stopping them for a second, making Sandy and Anna look at the camera. Both had puzzled expressions on their faces, as if Dad was disturbing two military strategists planning battle. Anna swears she remembers going right back to pulling Sandy's hair, trying to dunk her head under as soon as the photo was taken, Dad intervening and yelling at Anna to stop being the way she was. Sandy always wins any physical fights they have; Anna's the one who gets dunked, but, nevertheless, Anna likes to instigate most of their battles. The verbal fights are a different story altogether, and the outcome is never certain enough to place winning bets.

And Anna's trying to fight sleep right now because she wants to hear the next creak, the next step and pretend it's really only the house settling, feed her imagination more. Because she believes someone is out there right now even though it's been minutes since the last settling creak. If this is real, if there really is someone out there, why is Anna just sitting in bed thinking of her past, her brothers and sisters, her parents, thinking about everything else but the man on the back staircase. Why can't she do anything?

She's scared and she's trying not to scare herself more, but her mind works that way. She pictures the night breaking into pieces and a light shining through the darkness falling and she wonders if she's dreaming because she remembers speaking to Sandy across the room. She wants to warn her about the man on the stairs coming up silently, almost silently. Anna opens her mouth to speak while pushing the covers down to her pajama-covered knees so she can step to the ground in one quick motion. And the lockless door bursts open and the grinning man with the knife comes in one step and tilts his head in Anna's direction and she's too scared to do anything but quiver and choke back screams. He rushes to her twin sister's bed and Anna can't move or protect Sandy in any way or protect herself because she didn't hide under the bed or in the closet when she had the time to do so. All Anna can do is yell, but she can't because she's awake. And she doesn't want to wake everyone else up, not just yet. Sandy would start shouting and whining at Anna in the darkness. Sandy wouldn't realize right away that her sister was watching over her, trying to protect her.

Megan always watched her two sisters fight, wouldn't break them up, as if she could care less if they tore each other apart, and if Megan's also listening to the man on the back staircase as Anna is, Anna wonders if Megan's hoping he'll go to her sisters' room first; Anna wonders if Megan feels safe behind her locked door. Anna would. As a matter of fact, Megan was also in the second photo, barely visible in the faded background, but there she was standing behind the pool near the picnic table. Watching Sandy and Anna fight.

When this photo is passed around Mom says Megan has always wanted a twin to fight with, play with, and belong to.

Megan always protests: "I did not want another me."

But her face reddens and she takes the snapshot and throws it back into the cardboard box. In some ways Anna's glad Megan didn't get a twin because she is always telling her younger siblings what to do, and everything she does is right and she doesn't have to be compared with anyone else. But in another way Anna wishes Megan did have a twin so they'd have a perfect set: three sets of different cufflinks. Dad and Mom liked to joke about cufflinks a lot, especially when they and their kids were younger.

The locks are important because Anna wishes to God Sandy and she had put one on their door when they had the chance. Now it's too late and the man is breathing silently on the steps making plans. Anna can almost smell him, the scent of the woods he ran through to get to the highway and across the drainage ditch, the stench of the mildew and the dirt in the water on his pants legs, and Anna knows he really is there, waiting.

Anna was why . . . Anna was the reason why . . . what Anna did was the reason why her parents put a slide-bolt on their own bedroom door. Because she was so young and she didn't know what kind of sounds they were making and she really didn't care. All Anna knew was they were both home in one place and that she could tell on Sandy for ripping up the finger painting she made in third grade that day. Sandy shredded the construction paper on the school bus and Anna cried as she ran up the driveway, a curving hill, to her house, the same hill the man on the stairs crept up, passing like a shade over the bend in the driveway. Anna knew they were somewhere upstairs, her parents, because they weren't in the television room or the kitchen or the study and both cars were parked outside the garage filled with lawnmowers, rabbit hutches, still-unpacked boxes from the move to the country farmhouse life from their first in-town rental home on the other side of the incorporated line when they first arrived as a complete family from another university in Pennsylvania several years previously. So, Anna ran up the oriental carpet on the front staircase.

They didn't hear Anna coming. If she'd taken the back staircase, they would've had time to cover up. As it was, she stopped outside their door, shouted, "Mom," and barged into the room. Her tears quit instantly and her eyes widened.

It was such a strange thing for Anna to see back then, the first time she put things together in her young mind. It was like . . . Anna had never really thought about anything like this before. Her parents had never gotten into the duck pool naked like Megan.

Then it was Mom's turn to shout, "Anna!" She dropped her ripped finger painting on their off-white shag area rug. It lay there forgotten until later when her parents sat them all down on the living room couch and explained something about locked doors. And more, in vague terms, privacy, concept, love, knocking before entering closed doors, openness, order and then orders that must be obeyed.

Anna said, "But your door wasn't locked, and Sandy tore my picture on purpose . . ." And she made tears come again to see what they would add.

That was enough to get Sandy in trouble, and was the only thing that mattered. Dad put a slide-bolt on his door the next day. But that was then, the images of her parents disturbed expressions, their bodies entwined, the sheets spread across the back of the bed and looping onto the floor, and they're all a little bit older, and even though Sandy and Anna like to argue, they do get along.

Anna's thoughts catch in her mind as the past second repeats itself; a little while ago she swears she remembers arguing, pleading with Sandy again. She whispered: "Please get up, get up Sandy, he's right outside our door, on the staircase." Anna turns her head and swears she can hear the breathing, smell the rot on his tongue and Sandy won't wake up, get up, so Anna doesn't wait this time and climbs out from under the covers and wiggles beneath her bed alone before the door shatters and bursts open and the grinning man comes in looking for two girls soon to become teenagers and finds only one. Inside, Anna tells herself it's the right thing to do, the only thing she could do to save herself. Sandy wouldn't wake up and listen to Anna and it's all her own fault, and she's sorry Sandy, and Anna's shivering on top of her bed again even though she's pulled the blankets completely over her head and she's in utter darkness scaring herself silly thinking how she let Sandy down.

Sandy and Anna have shared the same room, crib, Mom's belly, since whenever. Sandy's bed is closer to the door, next to the white splotchy-painted bookshelves. Anna's bed is on the other side of the room, next to one of the windows over the front porch roof, facing the highway and the University's biological reserve beyond, the woods dark and chilling in the night's cold.

Anna remembers other restless nights, where she called out in the night and how Dad or Mom would come in and ask her if she was all right. The last time, only six months ago, when Anna was sneaking once more because of her age, after Anna saw that movie where all the babysitters end up slashed by a maniac who traveled through the night like a shadow, tinkling piano music drifting on dark wind, when she spent every weekend night babysitting and turning all the lights on bright until the adults came home, paid Anna for getting scared all alone in their strange houses, and drove her home late at night, her dark bedroom waiting for her, Sandy already asleep on her side of the room.

On some of these nights Anna would sneak out the window and crawl over the almost-flat roof shingles, hang her head over the roof's edge. Thinking: it's only twelve feet down. She was on the front porch roof, which sloped gently, and she wondered if she could reach down enough to slide to the ground on the white pillars that held the roof up. But she knew her body wouldn't twist enough. Then, once she knew she had no other choice, she'd pretend she was on the run. Anna had to jump, and she would in her mind. Without breaking an ankle, the fall would take her onto the grass and down the front hill, rolling all the way to the road. After she picked herself up, she'd be off.

And Anna knows she's thinking all of this when that someone on the back staircase takes another wicked step.

It sounds like a windblown rusty swing.

Halfway up now.

And if she's dreaming, Anna wants to wake up before the door bursts open again.

But she's not dreaming now and Anna's really scared herself this time because she swears she thought she heard another creak; the wind howling down the trees, and the windows shattering.

Sandy.

Wake up.

More than halfway up now.

And Anna wishes to God there was a lock on her door as she sits up in bed again, picks the blanket up by the edge, as silently as possible, and covers herself with it up to her eyes, the knuckles of her fingers hurting as they clutch the material. Swiftly, Anna drops the covers and opens the window to the front porch roof enough and sits back against the headboard. There're two more creaks on the back stairs, coming up faster now, and then another heavier sound as if that someone wants Anna to hear him stop three quarters of the way up, both feet on the same riser, and she's scared because Anna thinks he heard her open the window. Anna wants to warn Sandy, but she can't. He'd hear her and come faster, rushing through the only unlocked door on the second floor. And she stares at that unlocked door, then back at the open window, back and forth.

Wondering.

If she can make it onto the roof and jump for real this time without breaking her ankle, get to the neighbors before that someone becomes aware, the same someone who's almost to the landing now, who can see the door to this room straight ahead, who can see Anna through the door staring back at him, his face caught in the nightlight glow ... Anna holds onto her covers tighter than before and listens for the next telltale step, and if she hears it, and if she hears anything else, she's out on the roof.

Train Crash

As usual, I sit here on my bench and read the morning paper. Headline, Sports, Community News, Tempo; I even read the Food section in case I find something good to eat. I don't cook for myself, never could, but you don't know when you'll need to fend for yourself. It's almost one o'clock and the afternoon paper man fills the machine out front and lets the lid slam shut. I scowl at the man for disturbing my peace and quiet, but he's gone in a flash and probably didn't even see me through the reflective windows. Besides, I won't get up and buy one of his papers anyway; I only read the morning Press. And sit on my bench.

I read everything, even the classifieds, just in case. There are more kitchen designers wanted than regular working people. I was a carpenter by trade and there are a thousand of us out here. I don't have anything against designers, but somehow all the ads steam me up. I wish I had learned to be as capable with a pencil as I was with a hammer. I severed my right bicep completely and there's still a strange lump there where it's not supposed to be. Popeye would cringe. At the middle age point in my life the doctors told me they couldn't reattach the muscle and here I sit. After an hour I see the teenager across the station house, outside, watching the trains arrive and depart. He comes in every week or so and I can tell by the way he shuffles from bench to bench he wants to do more than watch; he seems to be looking for something he's lost; his eyes are searching, staring at the tracks. I act like I'm reading about the new plans for the city swimming pool while I watch him with slit eyes. No one could tell you I was doing anything more than just sitting there minding my own business. The teenager's bowlegged. He walks with a cool sway of the hips, as if he owns the world. I don't have anything against him. I keep to myself, but I notice how he stands up from his bench and walks inside. He studies the bulletin board, maps, photos of missing kids, teenagers, babies, adults, most of them women, and help wanted posted notes with ragged tags to tear off at the bottom. He pulls one of the phone-number tags for someone wanting cheap lawn mowing and then he works his meandering way closer to me and the ticket office. He slips the fortune-cookie size piece of paper into his scuffed blue jean front pocket before asking the frog-faced woman behind the ticket counter if she's ever seen a train crash. I'm close enough to hear them speak, but I still have to stretch; I shuffle a couple inches closer to the end of my bench. Folding my paper, trying not to rattle it too much. I think about secrets told when you think you're all alone, and safe, mistakenly believing you're with someone you can trust with your grievances.

The teenager takes a purple yo-yo out of his dull brown worker's coat pocket and swings it to the ground and up again. For a second I want him to come over and ask me the question. I can tell him a thing or two about trains, how a sudden, alarming brake around a curve sounds like trapped animals fighting each other in an illegal ring.

The woman stares at the teenager as if he was a muddy shoe on her carpet. She smirks at him the same way she smirks at me sometimes or at one of the many vagrants who sleep on the wooden benches outside the station. When she stares at me that way I want to tell her to get back to her own work, but I don't speak to her, ever. Who is she to look down at me? I like to read the paper here and she can't do anything about it. The boy's close enough for me to see little comma-shaped scars dotted along his face from ear to chin, and I know right away this is the teenager the morning manager has nicknamed, 'Pockface.' I like his nickname, and wish I had one so rugged and vicious, something I could defend, but I can tell the woman behind the counter could care less about him.

"You've got a home. Stop pestering me with stupid questions," the ticket woman says. She glances at the clock behind her and sighs.

Pockface shrugs his shoulders and gives her a wide smile. To me it looks genuine, but the woman is just able to hold her tongue. She looks like she's bottling up something explosive. He turns to me, to the left of the office window, and shows me how he makes his yo-yo go up and down. He says, "Watch this, Pops." The purple object begins to spin, once, twice, and then tangles.

When the string knots, he unravels it expertly and turns back to the woman, puts his elbows on the counter and says, "I'm doing a report."

Slapping papers together, binding the thin ones with a rubber band, the woman says, "I've seen you hanging around here."

"So. I'm collecting information for a school report." The teenager shrugs his shoulders again and glances at me. I rattle the Business section and quickly look down and then straight back at the boy. I want him to still come to me. If he asks me his questions he'll get a true answer and not words tinged with impatience and intolerance. In my day I was quite the storyteller. And I've seen and heard everything about trains and crashes, the way a train can pull from the front as well as the back, struggling titans, and what the conductor really has to control; everything he wants to learn and more.

Pockface brushes thin hair away from his eyes as someone comes up behind him.

"Can I help you?" The ticket woman looks past the teenager and then glances back, silently telling him to go. He steps to one side and watches as a pencil-thin, orange-haired woman moves up to the counter blowing gum bubbles. She snaps the gum back behind her magenta-smeared lips with sharp 'pop-skith' sounds. I know I've seen her before. She's always dressed like that, but there's something honest about her too this time, as if she's trying to break from her regular wardrobe. Once, after she had her hair cut short, she came up to me and asked if she could sit down. I made room, straightened my papers a bit, and told her to feel free. She seemed worried then and asked me if she looked pretty. I said, "Excuse me?" And she told me, "Men are all alike." She told me men couldn't answer any question directly, always had to be the ones in control, ask our questions first to change the subject. She said, "You're just like all the rest," then stood up and walked away.

"Got any cheap trains to L.A.? I need the cheapest." The frog-faced woman punches something into her desk computer while the woman chews her gum, turns to Pockface, who is now cleaning an ear with his pinky, and says, "I'm gonna be famous. You just wait. You saw me at the start and I always remember my friends. Tommy said I got what it takes. He said I've got star potential. He knows someone who works for that Hollywood talent show." Pockface opens his mouth to speak, but is cut off by the ticket woman.

"There's a train leaving at 7:30 tonight and another at 1:34 am."

Pockface twirls his yo-yo around and around.

"What's the price?" the woman asks.

"Both cost $192," the ticket woman replies.

I wonder if the orange-haired, would-be actress remembers me and the time she sat next to me, breathing heavily, as if she'd just raced down to the train station to ask me her questions and talk to me about men. She bows her head and moves back a pace, rummages through her enormous shiny silver purse for a second, and mumbles loudly enough for Frogface, Pockface and me to hear her. "I've got to call Tommy first. He'll tell me what to do." She glances at me and looks alarmed, eyes wide, as if she knows I couldn't help her if I tried. Moving away from the counter, she heads toward the exit doors, not acknowledging the bank of telephones along the far wall. A line of telephones no one seems to use in this cell age. I wonder if she lives close to me. She obviously can't find her own cell phone in her large bag, even though she's still trying as she walks away in a crooked path to the door. The door doesn't open when she presses the exit bar and she has to use all her spindly strength to heave it open. She's definitely thin enough to be an actress. She has that part down pat.

With newly cleaned ears, Pockface pops back in front of the counter, cocks a thumb at the gum-chewing woman, and says, "Can you believe that?"

I dislike people who overstep their bounds, become rude to get a laugh, and I know the boy is young and doesn't know the woman's situation specifically, but I still want to stand up, rush over and shake some sense into him. Rattle his smugness away. Teach him something about people and trains, how we each have our burdens. If he looks at me again I just might.

"She's no different from you," the ticket woman says and then clamps her jaw shut and stares at Pockface as if suddenly mummified or resigned, about to fold the largest mountain of laundry every day of her dingdong life.

"What do you mean, Lady? She's writing a report too?" the boy asks. I watch his eyes grow large and questioning and false.

The woman says, "You young kids think you're so funny."

"No we don't. I'm really doing work here. What's that lady's deal?"

The ticket woman glances at me. I pretend not to notice, and then she looks at her watch and says, "She comes in every week. Just like you do." Her tone rises in protective anger, as if the woman who left needs Frogface to stick up for her. The ticket woman's jaw twists, one cheek drooping lower than the other, and she's caught in a position she never expected to be in. I can tell she loathes the boy, and the woman, and wants to teach all of us a lesson. "Just like him." Without looking at her, I know she's pointing her finger at me and I want to scream at her to shut up. "Just like that man sitting by the revolving doors. Just like that old woman out front pacing back and forth. She takes a new train schedule every morning and throws it in the trash when she leaves at night. A waste of paper . . . if you ask me. What sets you and that woman apart from those others is that you and her come up to this counter to harass me."

Pockface glances down at his shoes, scuffed and bulging at the seams, and pockets his yo-yo before looking up again.

I could tell her there are two types here at the train station: those who talk and those who wait. I want to ask her what type she is because her speech confuses me. I stare at the boy again and find myself touching my face with my right hand, feeling the texture of my own cheek.

Pockface lightly taps the bell used to let the ticket woman know someone needs help. The bell emits a weak 'ding' and the woman swats his hand away.

The teenager retreats a step and says, "Then why didn't you tell her to stop pestering you with stupid questions, like you told me?" He folds his arms into his chest where they tighten and disappear in his jacket.

The ticket woman gazes at an incoming train, at the two couples waltzing onto the platform with their suitcases in hand, and says, "Because I feel sorry for her." Her eyes cloud over with kept-at-bay frailty and a surging pity. I can't see any color in them at all. I want to know if the woman will remember this moment.

The teenager stares at the ticket woman, and I can tell he sees the same thing I see: something itching to get out from beneath her frog features; the inflated jowls quiver on her jaw and her blotchy lips rub together like two mottled snakes.

"Well, we don't need your sympathy," the teenager scowls. My sense of pride rises but I somehow feel dishonest inside as if someone else has inhabited my body and taken over my mind. My fingers begin to twitch against the newspaper. The boy squares his shoulders and makes the woman again stiffen up her face.

Pockface backs away from the counter. His bowed legs move unevenly as the woman speaks out, "You're young. You have a future somewhere. She's young, but she knows she's getting older. She always comes in and asks what time the train to L.A. leaves. You haven't even chosen a destination yet." I rise two inches from my seat before I sit down again, and my fists tear my paper in half. They don't seem to notice the sound. I want to catch their attention, to focus on something really important. I want to yell out: Who made you so smart? You don't know anything. But I can't. I'd get a reputation for trouble, they'd make sure I wasn't allowed to stay on my bench, not even to read the morning paper, and it's the only place I can really call my own.

The teenager stops, stands and picks at his fingernails as the woman then says, "Go home. Go back to school. Just go. Leave me alone and stop pestering me." Her voice turns hard. "The next time I see you hanging around here, I'll call a cop on you."

Pockface shakes his head slowly back and forth as if someone has just told him a friend passed away and he won't accept it. I want to tell the woman she looks like a bullfrog, but instead I watch the boy turn and walk outside onto the platform near the rails. He glances up as a freight train roars past on the far track and then he heads in the direction of the pool hall down two blocks. As he's walking away I know he's still thinking about trains, wondering what a really big train crash would look like, the first car striking something twisted on the tracks and dragging the following cars off the rails, tumbling over on their sides with a world-stopping screech.

BONUS CONTENT

The first Chapter from Justin Bog's first novel, **Wake Me Up**, coming out in 2013:

Wake Me Up

By Justin Bog

CHAPTER 1

Near the end I no longer see the baseball bat, or, in the panic, keep track of who possesses it as they toss the bat to another ready, grasping hand. I trip into the bat at the exact instant when one of my classmates swings like a steroidal homerun hitter. I'm not saying I'm to blame either; even though my own anger propelled me into the street; I got in their way; I was in the wrong place at the wrong time. Of course, when the final blow splinters my skull I'm a gibbering mess and I blank out like a light, convulsing on the asphalt, bleeding from my ear, nose and arm; my elbow lays twisted like a pipe cleaner, my eyes flutter in spasm then close.

I have three days—the doctor says this, three days, nights, to watch my swelling brain struggle. They take a piece of my skull, a cutout—a surgical procedure I'd struggle with watching on one of those medical surgery shows if I had to watch. My mom would have no problem storing the clinical bloodbath away in her absorbed brain and also no problem teasing me about being so squeamish—a way to help relieve the swelling and cross their fingers. The worrying, secretive docs will keep me unconscious, they say, to help me get over the proverbial hump of pain and brutality. The surgeon tells my family, what's left of it, that at this point it's touch and go, up to God, up to fate. I hear this doctor's voice, spouting all around me in the pitch darkness, somehow, saying to leave my life to fate in his emotionless tone. He lacks a warm bedside manner, clipped formal medical jargon grating, short, barely able to say I'm sorry for your troubles before he leaves the waiting room.

* * *

Here's how it happened. My father, my mother, my father's lover, weren't there so how can I blame them—they were off pursuing their own dreams and demons and isn't life about running towards something? We all run. My parents moved us way out to Missoula, Montana following my mother's poetical yearnings. The University of Montana is the central, #1 with a bullet, economic force in Missoula. What happened to me, I can only imagine now in my dark chamber, may have happened anywhere, any town, USA. Bullies are born every single damn day. They seek popularity, belonging, a higher class social ranking, inevitably fall short and must take out their frustrations on somebody they perceive to be weaker—I've known several people with the bully placard hanging around their necks. I pity them.

Missoula, the Garden City, certainly has its fair share of frustrated teenagers. It's a university town, really a small Western city of close to 70,000 people near the Idaho border, the thin upper peninsula section, where mountains begin to rise up on all sides and clash to form Glacier National Park. This side of Montana is unlike the flat farmland and plains of the rest of the state. In junior high I had to do a report on a county in Montana, and got one of the farming blocks on the Eastern side of the state, Custer County, all dull 3,793 square miles of it—over 11,000 people at the time called Custer County home, the racial makeup 97% white and proud of it. The bulk of the people come from strong German and Norwegian descent. At least I have neighbors in Missoula who don't ride tractors or milk cows, not that there's anything wrong with that. I just know I'd make a terrible farmhand—and that I'd be teased just as equally by all the ranchers and their stolid rancher kids for being soft, clutching at my mother's hemline as she skins squirrels for stew. Missoula has a downtown center with low rise buildings that in some architect's noodlings try to look modern, a movie theater, a view of the mountains in the distance, a river that runs through it, decent restaurants and steakhouses, places to hide in, be alone with yourself, to engage with, or disengage; the perfect town for my family.

The four boys, the bullies from my high school, shout and laugh as they crack and shatter windows in the parked cars on the back road of this middle class neighborhood. People come out onto their dim, poorly lit porches too late, wary, after the damage is done, much too late, and the weakest of them will not venture further because of the sheeting rain and the threat of violence inherent in the sound of shattering windshield glass. Most of these adults shake their heads and think the world is going to hell in a hand basket; the kids vandalizing their street are all on drugs. Three of the vandals run faster than the fourth boy who doesn't want to run and is disinterested in catching up with his friends.

When I cross their path I'm already so angry. Angry—because of Deepika, her warm tea, cozy bungalow, the door my father knocked on—not because the boys are in my way and vandalizing cars; I could care less about the damage they're doing; deep inside I want them to ask me to join in, take up a rock and throw it through one of the Jeep windows. I'm angry with my father and the woman he was sexing up all last Spring; he'd gotten Deepika pregnant, acting just like one of these teenage thugs in front of me, and she never thought to tell him until today; she kept secrets like a fortune teller: only when convenient for her—the lies my father told Mom and I last April to cover this up. Weeks later I can see him begging my mother to let him back in the house: Let's become a family again. And she let him back. The weakness in her makes me even angrier.

I don't want to believe what's happening to my family. I've never had a death wish before. Thank God I haven't inherited that particular trait. I do want to live. I want to wake up.

Steaming, fists clenching, I enter the street shouting at the boys to stop—maybe because Ellis is one of them. I am a fool . . . believe he would somehow step up before any of them threw a punch.

I know I won't remember any of this if I even survive to wake up—and if and when I wake up I'm concentrating on this memory, trying so hard to get all of the details right—in case I'm questioned later by the police officer who tells my mother to get to the hospital quick. I'm fed up with my parents, and Deepika most of all; the child she will give birth to in the early part of next year, my future half-sibling; the rain, bracing and cold, saturates every piece of clothing I have on. I drip like a sponge. Then Ellis Pallino arrives, lagging behind his three buddies and causes my distraction and final destruction.

Are they all on drugs? Besides the teen pregnancy gossip with one of them, there's a rumor floating around school one of the three boys who circles me, baiting me, yelling, is going to bring a gun to homeroom. Look at the bullies now. They want revenge because someone started another rumor about the drugs they sell. Who could possibly predict they'd go off on me like a delayed bomb in the middle of a chilly, wet October evening? I never even speak to them at school, only pass them in the hallway and try to act invisible and small and unthreatening, a part of the background scenery, everyday wallpaper. All of them, except Ellis, are upperclassmen.

I don't understand why my anger pushes me to confront them. The largest one shouts at me: "Fag."

I'm stopped short by one awful word. To me it's worse than the other freaking F word. Has more hidden potency. It's not the first time someone has called me this. Again, in the school hallways, catcalls, you hear people using this word all the time, sometimes as real ribbing, sometimes just a catch-all insult not meant to offend too much, just joking, still unforgivable. In the rain I hear it and my stomach clenches and then tightens before they even punch me there.

His buddy chimes in: "Hey, shithead . . . faggot."

I couldn't think of anything to say, a stunned retort. The word lashes into me and I go mute, a rabbit stilled by a headlight. I definitely can't move by this time either. They circle around me, a new target. I try to keep all of them in my sight.

I'm not a faggot. I mean, how can they know I am when I'm not even fully aware of it myself. A denial for sure. Right here and now in the blackness. I deny it. I'm filled with so much self-hatred? Is that a lie?

Ellis steps into the picture too sudden and intense now. He's the strongest, smartest, hanging back. How could he be with them? Is he on drugs? I stare at him too long for the rest of them, which of course, dumbass, makes them feel uncomfortable—creeped out. I try to answer my own questions—see if his stare is blurry and diffuse—a pout, a parting of his lips I keep thinking about whenever we cross paths in school. His school baseball team hat shadows his face too much for me to tell, his long sideburns push through the haze, dark against the white of his chin. Yes, without speaking, it is freaking obvious I am attracted to Ellis. Crush city.

"What's the fag looking at?" The one hefting the baseball bat sneers, looks at his buddies to see if they see how threatening his sneer is, as I stare at Ellis. The leader's in Ellis's face—"You want this punk to be your girlfriend? You wanna be his boyfriend? You his boyfriend, Ellis?" The others whistle and hoot at me, calculated, annoying, aggressive comments splashing onto Ellis. I imagine Ellis's pale face turning red in the darkness.

I want to ask Ellis what he's doing with these guys— stop time. Don't you know they're crazy, violent dicks? That one of them used to string kittens up to a tree for batting practice? Is that the same bat? We just helped each other with algebra during lunch, and now there's rage and humiliation controlling his face, egging on group mindlessness.

"You like what you see?" The third boy joins the verbal assault. He's the one who grips the baseball bat, catching it as his friend tosses it to him in an arc through the air, choking up on the bat leaving five or six inches showing beneath his hand. He smacks the bat into his palm.

I know they're not putting me on; I've seen destruction and tripping and pushing in the school hallways; I usually shirk away or turn and take detours to the classroom I need to be in. I swerve around them like road kill.

If I knew how this situation would end for me I would've had enough guts to go back and laugh in their faces instead of acting scared. Being brave would be a new, invigorating feeling. I could do it now, but it's way too late for that kind of thinking. Why would they hit me? If I knew how to be strong why would they even pick on me; I hadn't given them a reason until they saw me staring at Ellis. People in the school hallways call each other fag, queer, sissy, and worse—no, there's nothing worse—all the time. I hear it all the time—directed at everyone—a universal putdown. No one—teacher, parent or principal—ever does anything to stop it. I hide in the closet because I know I'll never have the guts to come out, not in my school—that's my confession. I keep asking myself this time and time again; it becomes circular and devouring: why would they hit me so hard? Don't they know they could kill someone swinging the bat the way they do?

The name-calling breaks my stare and I get one more look into Ellis's shadowed face before one of them punches me in the stomach and I huddle over clutching from the blow. All my oxygen disappears and I stumble onto my knees sucking wind, spittle, and rain as the second bully hits me with the bat. I see it coming and try to deflect it with my right arm and the bat crushes my elbow and I see brilliant flecks and sparks of light and an overpowering blackness for a split second. The pain's enormous and I struggle to remain aware as the bat passes to someone else. I don't know who has the weapon now but when I open my eyes I'm on my knees searching for Ellis.

Earlier that very morning, I watched Ellis dress in gym class—not blatant about it either; I took covert, microsecond peeks, as all the kids bumbling about in the early morning did. His aloofness brought people to him, his good looks being judged on a higher scale—and not just by me; his newness was not off-putting; he made friends at an enviable rate. He's harmless, popular and untouchable. He used to be harmless and untouchable, but his popularity has changed to infamy in Missoula, and there are those who will always support this handsome boy no matter what. I did for the longest time.

It's Ellis who swings the bat last as I start to rise from the street, a shadow delivering the last blow. Someone else trips me; the blow alone shouldn't cause me to check out so completely. The four of them react by running away—now they're scared shitless. They run because they know this faggot bleeding on the ground means big trouble if they get caught, but why didn't they realize this when they started taunting me? Five seconds ago they could've stopped. The rage.

They run fast, the slap of their shoes echoes on the slick pavement.

In my last cogent moment, the bat swinging to crush, I have no doubt they want to kill me. I see this; I can call it an accident; I can rationalize the whole sorry mess away into something it's not because Ellis is there and doesn't really mean to betray me. We barely know each other anyway. I always try to keep to myself. I reign in any tendency to appear to the left of manliness, and the label of sissy has never really fit me anyway.

I'm a good actor whose ruse has cracked.

I've been found out.

I'm slipping away.

* * *

I speak to you from total blackness. I rest now in a private room on a hospital bed in the children's wing of a Missoula hospital. A security guard paces outside my room, up and down the hospital hallway. The press, local, soon to be national, is huge, foaming, vitriolic comments pouring forth as the days pass, candlelight vigils, a call for less violence, a peaceful mankind—a bleating, sickening new age twist of pablum from a certain segment, save the world, save yourself, find your inner broken child and relate to this poor poor poor child in darkness—we are all to blame. If

I could throw up, I would. The guard speaks to the nurses who flit back and forth delivering medicine and checking bedpans. Even though my eyes are closed I can see. Even though my ears are bandaged like a mummy I can hear. I know everything that's happening around me but I don't know why I know all of this. The word coma blinks there in neon, a truck-stop diner sign. Head injury. Severe brain trauma. I'm in a coma.

"He's comatose from the trauma to the brain." A doctor tells my mother this and encourages her to keep speaking to me to help make a connection: "It's so important that you try to continue any form of connection between you and Chris. Ask your family and church members to pray for Chris's awakening recovery." The doctor just assumes my family goes to church and carries the number of the hospital chaplain at the ready.

A presidential election is about to happen. We, my government class, the easygoing teacher—trying hard to remain objective (but we all know who he supports—and most teachers who want to keep their jobs are on his side)—the other stuck teachers, talk about it all the time. October. Fighting is in the air. Distorted into a tawdry back-and-forth. Polarizing, the most heated and harsh respond to anyone who is feared to be gay and I sink in my seat at the back of the classroom. Why should we let them marry? The teacher asks this since it's a huge component of the social issue war cycle between the two groups of disingenuous candidates, fomenting the fear. Here's why we shouldn't let Mo and Ho marry, says someone to my left, a mumble from another jock with issues . . . and these thoughts are there too.

* * *

I can see everything occurring at once. The past is the present to me and will merge with my unknown, blurry future. It's a strange, elevating experience because I can't prove this is happening. I hover within myself and outside myself, all at once, and time splits into a multifaceted gemstone. I lie on a thin mattress plumped up by pillows, prone and to the outside world totally unaware. I want to wake up. I want to hold my mother's hand even if she doesn't like anyone to touch her. I want to speak to my father but, of course, he's not here. I need someone to wake me up. Please. Odd—I'm not scared. I can't sense any panic within and this alone would terrify me if I could feel. I have a story to tell.

Somehow, the day after the attack I sense, I see, I am there watching as Deepika sits in her green Saab down in the hospital parking structure contemplating getting out of her car. She then walks into the hospital with her composure a bit off. There's no explanation why I am able to do this—I imagine a ghost feels like this and I know ghosts exist now . . . I am a wraith. It just is. Deepika's a few years younger than my mother, late thirties perhaps, but I've never been very good at guessing anyone's age. It's too late to sign me up for carny work. She's thinking about what she can possibly say to my mother in her defense if they happen to cross paths but she hasn't come up with anything of substance yet. Ghosts can read minds. Just kidding.

When I say 'she's thinking' I'm only guessing, but making a better than average guess since I, somehow, sense what compels people in my current state. Gift or curse? I'm the one in a coma. When someone says: I know what you're thinking. Or: You think you're so great, so smart, that person is only making guesses based on past behavior. Does this color how I tell my story? You be the judge. I know what you're thinking too.

Also, Deepika is thinking of her fictional characters, the ones she's writing short stories about back in her small, cozy office, about Sai and someone named Mrs. Plesher. She wants them to rise above conflict. She concentrates so hard on these characters during this time I picture her with multiple personality disorder. She's set a few of her stories in Sun Valley, Idaho, the ski resort, The Queen of the West.

Once, not too long ago, Deepika met her ex-husband, Andy, and his longtime companion, Terry, in Sun Valley over Presidents Week for a ski vacation. Terry was a bit too standoffish, only a wee bit officious, to warm up to Deepika (why be jealous of her—she wasn't a gay man—but, nevertheless, Andy and Deepika had once been married to each other, as short-lived as that union was, and Terry knew they still had a connection. Deepika did keep Andy's last name of Webber after the divorce, and the hotel clerk thought Andy and Deepika were still married, and Terry, terse and direct, snapped a bit too much and straightened the clerk's assumption out) and, after that trip, Deepika moved to Sun Valley, loved the blue sky, the 300 sunny days a year. She learned to snowboard, lived in the mountains for two years before taking the Visiting Writer teaching position, a two-year commitment, in Missoula at the University over a year ago, driving north along Idaho mountain roads to Montana. She learned all about Ketchum, the small mountain town that fed the Sun Valley resort economy, got a good feel for the character of the people there, the lay of the land, how white it is, the mountains in winter and the people too—how she stood out as an other. The most popular thing people said to her was: I wish there was an Indian restaurant here—using a tone of voice she questioned because it always sounded like they wanted her to whip up some Bombay potato curry, sag paneer, chicken tikka masala, and pick her brain about gods and Kali and the Dalai Lama—that's Tibet—easily confused, Buddha then? I'm Hindu. The whole town, the entire state, needed a boost in ethnic hospitality.

Deepika's main character, Sai, in her interconnected series of short stories she's tentatively titled *A Great Distance*, is gay, Hindu, but not from Calcutta. Sai was born in America to immigrant parents who wanted a better life but got a child instead. Deepika is driven to talk to the hospital's admittance desk attendant and find out how badly I was hurt; it's none of her business. It's not her fault either. Deepika remembers her ex-husband Andy and how he always complained to her about his family accepting all the blame because he turned out gay, as if they were martyrs, how sorry they felt for him having to live such a hard-knock life where everyone hates you because society thinks you're abnormal. I hope I can find out, wake up to knowledge just like Deepika, that straight parents and friends and acquaintances will try to blame themselves when a family member comes out of the closet, as if being gay somehow rubs off of them because of their actions or inattentions, the father isn't around enough, the mother is too smothering, distant, overbearing, emotionally distant or browbeating—don't forget to bring your umbrella, and, Chris, stop listening to that Nine Inch Nails crap and clean up your damn room—and, he has always been an overly sensitive boy—remember when he would run with his legs pumping but toes pointing way too high? Like a band majorette or something... his father saw that once and put a stop to it and the boy never ran again like that for fear he'd be labeled a sissy.

In Deepika's current writing I will have an influence so large I wonder if she'll dedicate her book to me. Her characters will be a channel for her own unacknowledged guilt and anger. When reality becomes fiction. Never become friends with storytellers because they will pick over your life like mockingbirds, take all the shiny bits. There will be too many similarities in Sai's memory wall, his fictional world of life and death: the four attackers who put me in the hospital will become three violent men and one disturbed woman in one of her stories—Ellis will be the woman—and all four of them will murder the put-upon mother, Sai's grandmother, in a grocery store in North, Georgia. It's Deepika's story—murderous violence, a defeating circle of parental hatred, a yearning to figure out why people act the way they do. And she appears so calm, hides her inner raging storm with beatific relish.

* * *

While I'm blinking into darkness, the bat rushing into temple and bone crunch, my father rests in the upstairs bath, a rectangular, white, deep, soaking bathtub. He hasn't filled the bath with water; he still has on the wrinkled suit he wore all the livelong day, the suit he slept in. I ran away hours ago and he's worried about me, for once, and not himself. But that worry doesn't stop him from drinking huge sips from the long large Grey Goose bottle and swallowing Tylenol one at a time with each vodka sting.

* * *

Somewhere else, my mother laughs as she picks up the Chinese food she promised for our dinner. A dinner we'll never eat as a family or otherwise. The cartons will sit on the kitchen counter and rot. The Chinese woman behind the counter has no way of foretelling this and she's overly friendly, twice asking if my mother wants chopsticks. Bowing thanks. My mother gives a small nod. Her body's still stiff, uncomfortable, and she barely manages the large bag filled with unread fortune cookies. The Chinese woman stops herself from asking if my mother needs help. But my mother's happy; there's an ironic cheer, rigid, contained.

* * *

Hours after the attack Ellis Pallino, his t-shirt stained a wet green, sits behind a gray metal table at the police station spilling his guts. I haunt him. My image is there behind his façade of eager helpfulness. At this very moment he tries to shift all the blame to the three redneck druggies he befriended at school because he's seen as a responsible type, good enough grades, popular, a future star of the football team, always helps his grandmother out of her wheelchair, anything he can say in his defense. His parents are also seen as the responsible types who do good things for the community. Well-connected blowhard dad's on the city council and was the one who took Ellis out of the private school he was attending and enrolled him in the public high school for his freshman year to make a good impression with his constituents. I never really met Ellis before the freshman year, but I'd see him around Missoula. Once, maybe twice, near the swimming pool or tubing down the river. He'd turn my head even then—I wanted to get to know him, but knew that would never happen—how wrong I was. We were all new to the high school . . . going from junior high to a much larger high school—trying to remain invisible. That's me. Get by. Ellis's father doesn't listen to him and doesn't want to hear the truth if it's really bad. His father tells him to come clean but blame the fuck out of the other three who are deadbeats and scofflaws with sealed juvenile records a mile long: firecrackers in mailboxes, animal cruelty—never proven—driving without a license, caught with marijuana, a joint or two, not enough to prosecute but enough to keep an eye on them, spray painting the new high school theater seats, two entire rows of them with archaic graffiti. Ellis's father knows the list goes on and on, privy to the information because of his political ties to the city, and, thinks: How the hell could my son be messed up with these three shits? Ellis folds under the persistent questioning, and knows the police don't believe a word he says even when he points to the other three who are then picked up systematically. When the others are questioned all three point the finger squarely back on Ellis and then on me, saying I came onto them, all at once, out on the street propositioning glass-shattering thugs for sex. All four of them are cunning liars and do it with so little effort it makes the lead detective's head spin into one of the worst mind-splitting headaches of his life.

* * *

Andy Webber watches Terry Elias, the man Andy calls his longtime companion, as Terry speaks on the wireless telephone in their small, yet striking in design, San Francisco Potrero Hill apartment—they spent their hard-earned ad-biz money making the living area ceilings barreled, gothic, a dream of Terry's from a childhood spent living in a home filled with arched doorways and circular windows, as if they lived in an ancient wine cellar, with repurposed farmhouse timber, curved and curious to anyone they invited over for a tasting of a discovered Pinot Noir. Terry listens to his mother, who lives in Las Vegas. She's forming a plan, trying to get her only son to fly down for the weekend to see a show—that sexy Zumanity thing would probably suit Andy, she says, a not-so-subtle jab, one of several left hanging. Terry and Andy both loathe Vegas. Andy wonders if she includes him in her plans. He's in love with her son. They even went so far as exchanging rings in a commitment ceremony two years ago on the lawn in front of The Palace Of Fine Art while California went through its own battle over their largest social issue: a union backed by the government.

He's now part of Terry's family. Terry moves out onto the balcony and Andy stares at his back and the Union Square city skyline in the far distance. He and Terry want to get married to each other for real, legally, and who knows, rumors in the city are flying this fall, San Francisco may yet get its act together and allow them to do so, but people still have to be convinced no harm will come when wedding bells ring for everyone.

Imagine that day.

Andy can't believe Washington State beat California to the altar.

Terry will get off the phone and act like his mother really cares and is accepting of the life she still says he's chosen to live.

Andy will say it's not a choice.

Terry will say his mother didn't mean it that way.

Andy will counter that his mother only tolerates them and is far from accepting and Andy will go so far as to say he is ready to not tolerate anyone who doesn't accept him for who he really is; he's sick of hiding; he did that once; he even got married once, divorced two years later.

That doesn't count, Terry replies. It was a marriage of convenience to a woman who wanted a green card and you were available.

She's a closer friend than that. There's never been an icy exchange between us (another barbed comment). We exchange Christmas cards. We're still close. I thought you liked her when you met Deepika on that ski trip?

How close can you really be when you don't even speak to her more than once a year?

Some friends you don't have to. I could pick up that phone right now, call Deepika, and she'd answer and we'd talk for hours, but you and I don't have time to argue about this anymore—you can go to Las Vegas without me if that's what your mother wants; I won't be insulted.

You will be.

Okay, but what if I try my hardest not to be?

* * *

Ms. Phyllis Deafers, well into her sixties, snoozes in the teacher's lounge the morning after I'm beaten to a pulp. She doesn't remember me from study hall where she monitors the room like a weary battleship. No one remembers me; I'm only a freshman, but after the principal requires a moment of silence in my honor, the whole class body tries to remember who I am, and most fail. That won't stop the most savvy and college-bound from coming up with plans for candlelit vigils and bake sales to help defray hospital costs and the pleas and testimonials will rise daily as my coma deepens: I'll have many best friends recalling how they passed me in the halls, helped me with my homework, cut class with me, pumping my loner image into school rebel territory. Ms. Phyllis Deafers will fall asleep that night watching Jeopardy without being able to answer anything in the form of a question.

* * *

Amos Morataki, a classmate who blurts out his innermost thoughts to me, who knows I barely listen, is at home the evening of the attack. He was even gloating, just the littlest bit in his tone, about my father at school today until he saw how his words struck me: It's too bad your father lost his job—telling me something I didn't even know, set me off on a path leading to my own destruction. I wanted to flee the school, get home, to witness my father lie to my face again. Was Amos the catalyst? Amos can tell I didn't have a clue my father had been lying to me about work, to Mom, still dressing every morning in his false and battered suits. Amos won't even know about my hospitalization until the next day at school when the principal makes the announcement over the P.A. system during homeroom. The principal's tone will be practiced sadness with a hint of resignation and the creeping worry of lawsuits. Later, when the eyewitness account rises, he'll check with the superintendent about the school's position on the protection of gay students and where liability lines are crossed. Is the school to blame for not protecting me? Is it a hate crime like the newspapers suggest in bold print, emblazoned across the front page? Another desert State wants to do away with all bullying protocols in public schools because their right marching guard says protecting gay kids means the schools condone the gay lifestyle of these same gay kids. Take the protection away. Other kids are bullied, why single out them?

* * *

Mary Follick sits in another cubicle at police headquarters spilling her guts, crying and hysterical until her parents arrive. She witnessed the fight and the end of the attack as the boys took off. Mary knows the name of two of the attackers and heard what they were calling me—she'll never forget it for the rest of her days—and would tattle all of this to the reporters outside in the rain three hours later.

Did you know the injured boy?

Yes.

Did you know he was gay?

No. Wait. He never said he was gay. They called him fag. Maybe he's still in the closet. I didn't talk to him much. Liar. Smug with a self-important air of satisfaction Mary will reveal she has always suspected I am gay. I wouldn't go to the seventh-grade dance with her, she says to the reporter, and this is her proof. She kept chasing me and chasing me until I left the dance, frustrated.

Mary hands the detective her cell phone, one of the off brands, not an iPhone, that takes bad quality digital pictures. She explains how to forward the photos she took in a panic while behind the car, hiding from the fight. The detective smiles. The case is wrapping itself up. In one of the snapshots, through the rain glimmering like a sheet reflecting the streetlamps, the baseball bat is blurry, highlighted in mid-swing, in the hands of a kid with long sideburns, a trucker hat shadowing his face—still too dark to rely on in court, but not blurry enough to show to Ellis and start a teary confession that will last for years.

From Mary they get the names of two of the attackers. She doesn't tell the police these two boys call her slut, ho, make moist kissing sounds as she drifts close. Whenever she passes them in the hallways of the school they make her feel like shit. Ellis has never called her anything. She can't believe Ellis was an active participant and imagines him frying in an electric chair wearing an orange jumpsuit, heavily tattooed and bald as an eagle. He'd deserve it if I die, she thinks, and for once I'm in her corner rooting her ire on.

* * *

Edy Augustyn, Ellis Pallino's biology lab partner, finds herself alone in class the day after the attack. No one will be her biology partner now as if she tainted Ellis somehow. The minds of teenagers, all the stupid decisions made everyday, never amuse me. She sits behind the black counter and asks the teacher if she can join Mary Follick—who is also alone, branded a different kind of traitor—if he'll place both of them together, since I'm now in a coma and won't be coming back anytime soon. There isn't any delicacy in her voice; she just wants help with all the lab work and will beg and mewl until she gets her way. I'm not coming back. No freaking way.

* * *

At the same time I fight for consciousness, beaten to within an inch ... Dr. Fusil waits for the results of my mother's blood tests, as we all wait, as everyone in my family waited in separate areas of the hospital: a terrible coincidence? Fate? My mother and I, my father too, if you count his crazy bullshit maneuver that got him locked up; he's the only one who has an ugly death wish. Lock him up and throw away the key. Too much of a coincidence? It happens. When more than one person is sick in a family, or hurt, or undergoing psychiatric evaluations, which just about covers us. If I was able to speak, move, I would high-five my mother on the way to get a CT, join the party. My sense of humor isn't that cruel. I know this isn't funny. The doctor, my mother's ER doc, even though she's only three years out of medical school, knows the tests won't reveal anything. Dr. Fusil has to run the tests, cover every little step, but what she's most interested in is the MRI and what she intuitively knows will show up on the films: the little black spots. She remains upbeat and positive when she's around my mother waiting for the shoe to fall after she tells Maddy what she doesn't want to hear. With everything around her collapsing the last thing my mother wants to hear is: take care of yourself—she's been distracted and involved with herself for too long now.

* * *

Travis searches his apartment for a blank greeting card he bought at Target. He's composing a sympathy card for my mother, for the hardship she's now going through, for the way he can be there for her if she'll only open her eyes. He senses her sadness and wants to help her if not for all the right reasons. He sits at his kitchen table with the card and can't think of an opening line.

* * *

In Boston, Deepika's brother, Ananda, sits in his Medical Clinic office going over charts. One of his patients, a woman who started bleeding in her stomach lining, almost fainted, and needed four pints of blood, is in full recovery. Ulcer.

The woman's husband says: She is a lucky woman.

She says in reply, with a tinge of cynical irony: I'm on my second life now.

Ananda says to them both: I firmly believe in fate. Please don't fear anything. Things come and things go.

Deepika would roll her eyes and tell her brother he's laying it on a bit thick.

The man and the woman don't have anything to add.

Ananda thinks about his sister, Deepika, and the child she carries, worries and joins his easy-going philosophy to her situation. He's trying hard not to judge her. This is her fate.

* * *

Liv opens her University Logo Shoppe, a place to buy University of Montana kitsch of all shape and form, Team Spirit candles set into little log cabins with U of M written on the sides, ceramic grizzly bears in school colors, copper, silver and gold, stemming from Montana's history of mining, although maroon, because it's easier to duplicate and print, became the official substitute for copper in the early nineties and no one ever remembers this fact—

We Are The Grizzlies—shot glasses with clever sayings, silver jewelry from Bali, multi-colored scarves, t-shirts and hoodies with school emblems blazing. Liv calls Deepika the morning after the attack to set up a meeting for tea in the late afternoon. Just the daily ritual Liv goes through, walking through the campus center to her little store, saying hello to the other shop owners on her street, griping about the morning's headline, some boy from the local high school in critical condition at the hospital, what a shame something like this is happening in her city. Deepika tells Liv she can meet later after subbing for my mother—the gods and goddesses at intricate play. Of course she doesn't tell Liv that sticky gem, and Liv can sense Deepika's departure—one of these days, soon now, Deepika will say an un-teary goodbye to her and Montana and never looking back and never return—Liv won't cry either. She never does. A campus population is too transient to shed tears over. Deepika and Liv make a point of meeting once, twice, sometimes more times, a week to talk and enjoy each other's company ever since Deepika met Liv when Deepika signed the first rent check on one of the five small rental homes Liv owns in and around Missoula. They made fast friends and laugh untethered and sometimes louder than either of them knew they could laugh—they bring out a rich sense of camaraderie, a sisterhood. Deepika has been gone most of the summer and only returned, with child and showing, to finish her book, and, because of her pregnancy, asks to be let out early from her last winter term teaching obligation. Liv hasn't even asked Deepika about the baby. She'll get around to it.

* * *

Doctor Gapestill, my neurosurgeon, stops his rounds to check on me almost every hour. He worries and frets and consults other specialists about my progress and has upgraded my condition to beyond critical. The swelling will not go down and this really concerns him. The night after my attack, post brain swelling surgery, skull removal, after spending one whole 24-hour period in a coma, after Doctor Gapestill rechecks the settings on the respirator because my breathing is even more labored, something blocking my airway, the doctor will inform the media of this sudden downward change and they'll go off and write it up for tomorrow's story. CONDITION STILL CRITICAL FOR BOY IN COMA. Doctors fear the worst. The spin will be negative and depressing and I'm lying in blackness living with the knowledge I could die. The day after that the headline will read: HATE CRIME HITS MISSOULA. The police involved in my case will cringe and follow procedure. Everyone will think they're not doing enough and make them feel hollow. That second night hundreds of University students, teachers, high school parents and their children will hold a candlelight vigil outside the hospital—let us shine a light on hatred so ingrained it makes all of us culpable. Pray for me. Hold your light higher. Bring me out of the darkness of hatred. The light of innocence will shine when I open my eyes. My ass.

* * *

At the moment an image comes to me of a complete stranger, a man named Harry—the psychiatric nurse who will take care of my father—is sleeping so he can get up early for his day shift. I won't be able to sleep until I wake up. When Harry does wake up he'll wonder which patient he'll have to shut up today—I want to tell him, but why ruin his expectations. Who he'll have to yell at, who will scream at him, who will give him trouble about taking the medication and who will try to play him and Harry's thoughts always circulate this way upon waking and getting ready for work. The Psych Ward is full of manipulation and deceit; Harry wants to always remember this, and that includes the doctors on staff.

* * *

Lance and Sheila sit at the Detroit airport waiting for their flight number to be called. They don't know the specifics of what my father spoke about but they're worn and very willing to see what kind of trouble my father has gotten into. My father practically begs Lance to fly out and save him. They really just want to help even though my mother tried to put them off the day before when Lance called full of concern for my father and his lost job. They weren't really my mother's friends to begin with, my mother having that learned iciness so hard to thaw, and she knows they wouldn't really lift a finger if pressed, if the shite really hit the fan, that they're consumed by their own social-ladder climbing, and lack an attentive listener's tact. But at least they are making the flight out, someone who is like a brother to them is in need, and arrive the night after my attack, bursting to take charge of the situation; there's nothing they can do; they're stuck in the waiting room with all the rest. I think my mother will let them try to take over if only to see how they fight for control with Nell.

* * *

The night of the attack my mother's only sibling, Rhea, is watching the news with her husband. She's following the election like a bee after honey. It's three weeks to the Presidential election and she lives in red San Diego County. Her two kids play in the backyard with the neighbor kids. Her first real housewives dirty martini hasn't loosened her up a stitch and she's bitterly complaining about both candidates whenever one or the other appears on the television screen. She asks her husband, Carl, to make her another drink. He goes to the bar to do so and hears Rhea's running commentary on the state of the nation from the kitchen. Carl shakes the martinis. Rhea, Carl, and their kids will speak to Nadine, mom's best friend, the next day. Rhea is mom's younger sister. Rhea will get off the telephone after hearing about me and start ripping into my mother and her character and how holier-than-thou she's always been. Carl will ask if she wants to take a flight to Missoula and Rhea will contemplate this all night before deciding to wait until she hears from her parents, my grandparents, Millie and Frank.

* * *

Mrs. Gallows sits and reads her student English compositions the night of my attack and rolls her eyes and points out the misspellings to her husband time and time again; there are so many.

* * *

Mr. Roffiger, the algebra teacher, sits at his kitchen table with all of his children, he named all of them so he isn't at a loss at remembering how each of them came into his life, eight and counting. His wife serves grilled cheese sandwiches and iceberg salad with under-ripe tomatoes and they say a prayer. He thinks of the tests he has to grade after dinner and with a twinkle in his eye listens to his youngest as she tells a knock-knock joke. He won't remember my absence from class until he finds out he has no test from me in his stack of papers. He'll then wonder where I was and why I wasn't in school; I'm one of his stalwarts, one of the kids who doesn't need to practice more and more just to get things right. He'll mutter and cluck when and if I reappear in class and, in front of everyone, give me a demerit for missing the math team quiz, as if I don't have enough on my plate. Maybe I won't even go back to school; I have the biggest excuse in the world not to.

* * *

Millie and Frank, my mother's parents, are driving through Alabama in their used Winnebago Ultimate Advantage with rose accents and cherry wood interior trim. They just stayed in Gulf Shores, Alabama for a week at the Gulf Shores State Park where Millie took a picture of Frank in front of the sign that says: Please Don't Feed Or Aggravate The Alligators. They've been on the road for two months and are ready to get back home to Ohio. They're not prepared for the news of the attack the next day when Nadine calls them from the hospital. They're just one of many family members Nadine shakily calls from the hallway in the hospital's children's wing. They'll make plans to beeline-it home to New Albany; take a flight out of Columbus with two connecting flights in Minnesota and Salt Lake. At least they'll arrive on the second day of my forced sleep.

* * *

Glynnis, my dad's former personal assistant, doesn't have a clue about what's happened to my dad or me, but when the newspaper arrives on her doorstep the next morning she'll head straight for the office with tears at the ready. He was such a good man, she'll justifiably pronounce, and all this tragedy is such a shame, shame, a crying shame. What a poor, poor boy. She'll ask my father's former partners if the law firm should send flowers or not . . . to be tacky and righteous or not to be? In an interdepartmental memo they'll okay the flowers, short, to-the-point embarrassment.

* * *

In this growing Greek chorus—these lives I am forced to witness like a moving picture, a shuffling not-so-chronological film of intersecting characters—most of whom I don't know; and the ones I do know I realize I didn't know at all—Valeria Brandow takes off all of her clothes five hours after my attack and streaks into the drizzling, Missoula, Montana, October nighttime chill. The police pick her up, wrap a blanket around her shivering, wet, naked body, and take her to the same hospital where I lie sleeping. The doctor in the E.R. will try to send her up to the Psych Ward for an evaluation. The Emergency Room nurse will call Valeria's sister, Nancy Followatta, listed in the computer system as an emergency contact person (Valeria's been there many times), to come get her when they find out Valeria's insurance won't cover the locked, overnight stay. Nancy will end up taking Valeria home with a sour promise to the police she won't allow Valeria to do this again.

The police will shake their heads and tell Nancy her sister could end up in jail if it does happen again. The Missoula police have a long file on Valeria listing similar episodes but their hands are tied; they want to do the right thing but don't have the heart.

Nancy glares at Valeria on the short car ride home, berating her, and finally touches her hair, as if petting the fur of her favorite pet, and says: Val, this has to stop. I can't take it anymore. You have to take your medicine.

Valeria has long since stopped caring about taking anything anymore.

* * *

Along with his partner, Officer Pardue, Officer Ken St. Amour will end his night filling out all the paperwork on my case and my father's. It will take him three extra hours to get everything down to his satisfaction. He is spent after he checks out and heads to a bar frequented by off-duty police officers. They ask him if the fag will live, but they don't mean it as a slur; it's just the way some of the older cops talk. Officer Ken St. Amour starts to get angry; he doesn't show it as he drinks another draft. He knows he won't sleep well and he'll be jumpy all day at work tomorrow. He orders a shot of tequila for Officer Pardue when he arrives and waits for the bartender to tell him a new joke.

* * *

Mr. Abrassini, a colleague of my mother's at the university, hears the news like everybody else the next day over coffee. He reads the paper with a sense of righteousness and entitlement. He thinks my mother is getting knocked down a peg, a just thing; because he doesn't like her writing at all, doesn't get her poetic stance (he hasn't produced anything of merit in a long, long time) and she gets more respect than he ever will.

* * *

Marjolaine, the University of Missoula English Teaching Coordinator, sits in her office the night of the attack and tries to get her desk in order. She thinks if she can just work three more years she'll get her pension and be able to leave Missoula for a better place. She hates the winters and her joints ache and she believes everyone in the department makes fun of her behind her back. She'll be left out of the loop on my attack and what's happened to my mother, but she'll put a happy face on and try to coordinate all of the class schedules so that my mother, if she misses a lot of them, won't suffer for it.

* * *

Nell, my father's only sibling, will not be called until the day after my attack. A no-nonsense type, she will want to know everything, and Nadine will try to tell her but Nell won't have any of it. She'll hang up on Nadine and book a flight from Palm Springs the next instant. Then she'll call her neighbor and say, Reggie, you're going to have to look after the dogs and don't overwater my orchids. Nell's on her way, Nadine will tell my mother as she sits at my bedside. My mother and Nadine both roll their eyes and try to talk me awake. My mother will kiss my face like sleeping beauty but I won't wake up.

* * *

The Chess King, my father's father, my absent grandfather, will be traveling back home from London. He's in his eighties, but fit as a fiddle, and I don't remember ever meeting him. I must have way back when. I was just a toddler, perhaps. While in the UK my grandfather visits old friends from the fifties, friends who stood up for him at his wedding long ago. He plays chess for a month with a lot of the genius-level chess players and then books a flight to New York City after spending another week of solitude roaming the coffee shops and Indian restaurants on London's West End. He hasn't spoken to my father in well over ten years, since his wife died—my dad never mentions his mother or her death from high cholesterol and blocked arteries. The Chess King knows his son lives in Montana because Nell keeps him informed but he's too stubborn to interrupt his son's life any more. He's already done enough of that for one lifetime. On the flight back to the states The Chess King amuses the flight attendants by making up dirty limericks using their first names: There was a young lady named Cheryl_____.

* * *

I see all of these people. They're living and breathing and acting on their basest impulses. I lay in a coma. They live. I hover over all of them, all at once. I can see my body, motionless, wired up, adrift. And I can find out why this happened. This is my story and I won't remember any of it when—if—I wake up. But I'll try to remember—I'll try damn hard.

Please continue reading more of the story of **Wake Me Up** in 2013.

If you enjoyed **Sandcastle and Other Stories**, please tell your friends to read the tales too. I love to hear from readers so please don't hesitate to share your thoughts.

ACKNOWLEDGEMENTS

To publish any book is a huge endeavor. The time flew by. I remember long ago thinking that writing a book was the hard part. Boy, was I wrong. So many people helped bring **Sandcastle and Other Stories** to life and often joined in hatching this newly published form, and I want to acknowledge them here.

Kari Hock—for seeing that needle in the haystack and giving **Sandcastle and Other Stories** and my writing a fighting chance out there in the huge world of books. Wishing great things for Kari and Green Darner Press.

Carl Christian—I thank you. You gave me a needed boost in the writing life with your great e-magazine, **In Classic Style**. I love you and your singular zest for life. Find Carl on Twitter @ inclassicstyle and subscribe at www.inclassicstyle.com.

Dee Solberg, your writing life is growing and your story of Angus and Lilly has captivated me. Thank you for being an early reader—editing, and then reading some more. Your comments help me see the work in a different way. Find Dee on Twitter @ Wxmouse and read her writing on her blog www.ramble-inn.blogspot.com.

Dionne Lister is an Australian writer and an early reader too. Look for her fantasy novel, **Shadows of the Realm** and **Dark**

Spaces. Dionne is one member of the hilarious duo that makes up the writer-centric podcast TweepNation. I look to Dionne for much laughter, wise counsel and grammatical-error busting. Find Dionne on Twitter @DionneLister & @TweepNation and follow her blog www.dionnelisterwriter.wordpress.com.

Amber Jerome~Norrgard is a poet and author—check out her first book of poetry **The Color of Dawn** and her nonfiction book **4 a.m.**—who has become entwined in my writing life and continues to amaze me with her passionate support of writers and the craft. She is also the cohost of the TweepNation podcast.

Rachel Thompson is the #1 author of two books, **A Walk in the Snark** & **The Mancode: Exposed**, and the forthcoming **Broken Pieces**. Rachel helped me learn a bit on the marketing side of the book business with her own Social Media Consulting business Bad Redhead Media. Find Rachel on Twitter @RachelintheOC or @BadRedheadMedia and on her blog at www.rachelintheoc.com.

Jane Isaac is a fellow author whose first mystery novel, **An Unfamiliar Murder**, is not to be missed. Find Jane on Twitter @JaneIsaacAuthor and follow her blog www.janeisaac.co.uk.

Kriss Morton is a huge supporter of authors on the front lines and she is a bacon wizard. Follow her on Twitter @AKMamma and discover her blog at www.cabingoddess.com.

I also thank Richard Bach, author of **Jonathan Livingston Seagull**, who was kind enough to read my writing over the past year before publication and gave me the inner belief to take a leap forward to publication. My writing life is richer for his wise counsel. Check in on Richard at www.richardbach.com.

I can't imagine moving forward without thanking Sabryna Bach, the author of **Red Delicious**, whose passionate support of writers knows no bounds.

And Chris, I thank you always for your love and kindness. Your gift of free tech support for life sure did come in handy—I kept that birthday card and it hangs on my wall next to my computer. This book wouldn't be here without you and your guidance. Love.

ABOUT THE AUTHOR

Justin Bog makes his home in the Pacific Northwest with his partner of almost 25 years. He received an English degree from the University of Michigan, and an MFA in Fiction from Bowling Green State University. When not writing, he spends most of his time looking after two long coat German shepherds, Zippy & Kipling, and two barn cats, Ajax The Gray & Eartha Kitt'n (she has a secret she wants to tell you).

Visit Justin at his A Writer's Life blog: www.justinbog.com.

Follow Justin on Twitter @JustinBog.

You can also find Justin Bog's Author Page on Facebook: https://www.facebook.com/JustinBog1.

Address: 1004 Commercial Ave, #480
Anacortes, WA 98221

You can email Justin at Justinbog@me.com.

Feel free to contact Justin through any of these communication routes and let him know what you thought of **Sandcastle and Other Stories**.

CPSIA information can be obtained at www.ICGtesting.com
Printed in the USA
LVOW041509070213

319136LV00011B/1215/P

9 780988 478411